Stranger Than Fish

short stories

by J. E. Hardy

*For Mother —
This took long enough —
Love Joo.*

Published in 1989 by ONLYWOMEN PRESS, Ltd.,
radical feminist and lesbian publishers,
38 Mount Pleasant, London WC1X 0AP

Copyright © J. E. Hardy.

"Old Photographs" and "The Party Game" were first
published in *The Reach: lesbian feminist fiction*, edited by
Lilian Mohin and Sheila Shulman, Onlywomen Press,
London, 1984. "Stella and Clarissa" was first published in
The Pied Piper: lesbian feminist fiction, edited by Anna
Livia and Lilian Mohin, Onlywomen Press, London, 1989.

All rights reserved. No part of this book may be reproduced
in any form or by any method without the written
permission of Onlywomen Press, Limited.

Cover illustration © Ingrid Rafael.

Printed and bound in Denmark by Norhaven.
Typeset by Columns, Reading, Berkshire, UK.

British Library Cataloguing in Publication Data
Hardy, J.E., 1958–
  Stranger than fish.
  I. Title
  823'.914 [F]

ISBN 0–906500–32–X

For my grandmother, whom I loved very much

J. E. Hardy is thirty years old and lives in Plymouth. She has been gainfully or otherwise employed in a number of jobs: cleaner, cook, tutor, labourer and travelling fishmonger to name a few. She now works as a sub-editor of academic texts and occasionally yearns for a large cod and an axe.

Contents

Stranger Than Fish	1
Old Photographs	35
Stella and Clarissa	48
Pen the Runt	85
The Party Game	108
Avocadoes for Breakfast	117
Spit in the Desert	124
Robert and Helen on the Rocks	142
Less of the Spaghetti Legs	161

Stranger Than Fish*

1

Axel walked into Sainte-Croix-de-Mont in the enervating, white-light of the mid-day heat in mid-July. She paused at the gates to the estate, lowering her rucksack from her aching back. It had been a seven-mile walk from the station in Cadillac, along pitted, dusty roads, hemmed in by vines. She had not been sure that she was walking the right roads, growing thirstier by the yard, unable to ask for directions, for water, for the time. Then she had seen the drive to the château, flanked by austere, flaking pillars, and there, behind the leaves of a wild vine, she had seen the faintest etching, the letters becoming shallower with each generation: Guillot. She had arrived, a day and a half after leaving London. She had never seen anything as graceful, as delapidated, as faint – as magical – as Juliette Guillot's château.

Axel pushed her hair back, wiped the sweat from her face and neck with the hem of her t-shirt, heaved her rucksack onto her back once more and started the long, crunching walk up the driveway, lined, had she known it, with Judas trees.

'Ah, Mademoiselle Axel, n'est çe pas?' asked the woman at the door. Axel smiled nervously, embarrassed by her dusty, dirty appearance. 'Je suis Madame

Gautier, la cuisinière ... Entrez, venez donc.' Madame Gautier beckoned Axel into the dark hall, pitch black after the dazzling sunlight of the afternoon. Axel moved awkwardly in the darkness and jostled the woman closing the door. 'I must apologise for Madame Guillot. She is shopping at the moment, for we expected you to call from the station and then we thought we must have the dates muddled up. But she shouldn't be long, she has only gone to Cadillac. Anyway, I must show you your room and let you wash and rest or whatever you would like to do. Was it a long trip? Why didn't you call from the station?'

Axel had become accustomed to the gloom and realised by Madame Gautier's expression that she was being asked a question. 'Um.' She twisted the strap of her rucksack and frowned, sweating. 'Um ... I don't speak French. I'm sorry.'

'Comment?'

'Um ...' Axel dug deep in her mind, trying to recall the phrases of her early schooldays. 'Um ... je ne com ... comprender pas?'

'Ah – you don't understand. Maybe I am speaking too fast. I am sorry. Is this any better?'

Again Axel knew she was being asked a question. Again she shrugged and sweated, wanting to be away, outside, home, swimming, asleep. Indeed, anywhere but in this darkened hall with this well-meaning woman who made no sense. She became aware of her own lank, dirty hair.

'You don't understand anything? Nothing at all? Nothing?' Madame Gautier cut the air with her reddened hands.

'Rien,' echoed Axel falteringly.

'Oh la la.' The cook tutted and shook her head. Using sign language she guided Axel up the stairs to her room. Axel, being nervous, was unsmiling and clumsy. She thanked Madame Gautier in English and waited until the door had closed to look around.

The room she found herself in was large and bare. The walls white-washed stone, the floor bare planks, the bed a large, lumpy four-poster, the wardrobe a leaning oak monolith. Dropping her rucksack on the bed she crossed the room and opened double doors in the corner to find a bathroom with a huge claw-footed enamel bath, a small scallop-shaped sink and a spotted mirror, with the same white-washed walls. She walked back to the bedroom, over to the window and threw open the shutters. She did not know then that she could see the whole Guillot estate spread out before her, the outlying farms and the vineyards; the yard and pressing rooms below her, the cellars and out-houses, a land which spread to the chalk escarpment overlooking the Garonne, a land which had grown with the Guillot family over centuries. She started to smile when she glimpsed the river bisecting the land. She turned away to rummage through her clothes and, having found her shorts, crept out of the room and down the stairs, not wanting to listen to more French.

Whilst Axel swam in the river, Juliette arrived home and told Hugo to unload her car as she went to the kitchen for coffee.

'Madame Gautier, I have bought everything you asked for, although I do not understand what you can possibly do with it all. Also I saw that detestable man, Monsieur Rouget, who tells me that I must pay two per cent more this year for property management, although I cannot imagine why. I must have coffee and, I think, a small cognac.' Juliette sank into a chair and fanned herself with a newspaper. 'And it is too hot. I have never known weather like this in July. It wears one out.'

'The girl has arrived.'

'What?' Juliette stopped her fanning.

'The girl, what is her name? Alex? No, Axel; she has arrived.'

'Alexandria's daughter is here is she? Why did she not ring from the station? How did she get here?'

'I do not know. She speaks no French.'

'Oh, ennuyeux ça. No sooner do you start doing a favour than it starts to go wrong. No doubt she did not ring from the station because she could not.' Juliette sipped her brandy and pulled out her cigarettes.

'Why did you ask her to stay here?' asked the cook,

moving around the kitchen, putting provisions in cupboards.

'I did not ask her! Alexandria – you know, Michelle's daughter – she called me and said that she thought a few months working and living here would do Axel good. Apparently she has just finished her Baccalauréat or whatever they have in England and needs a change. Well, with a name such as Axel, what chance does she have?' Juliette lit the cigarette that had been dangling between her fingers. 'Anyway, where is she?'

'Asleep I should think Madame. I took her to her room and I have not seen her since.'

Axel was pulling herself out on to the river bank, tired and dripping. She collected her clothes and walked back to the house in the distance, the sun warming her as she trod the straight lines of vines.

'What is she like, this Axel?' asked Juliette, crossing her legs with a rustle of silk.

'English.'

'Madame Gautier you can do better than that, even in this heat.' Juliette dabbed her lips with the back of her hand.

'She is tall and big, like a German. She was very dirty, but I suppose she had been on trains. She had greasy hair and was very clumsy.'

'Marvellous – just what I need at the moment. A mute, dirty Leviathan.'

'She has the most beautiful eyes, they're different colours, dazzling,' said the cook, feeling she had been a little harsh.

'Madame Gautier, I have to feed and be pleasant to this girl for months. I do not think her eyes alone will repay me.' Juliette finished her drink and stretched. 'Well, I shall leave her to sleep, it will mean a few hours of reprieve.'

Axel climbed the stairs with stealth and tip-toed into her room, hearing voices in the kitchen. She swept her rucksack to the floor and pulled off her wet clothes before tumbling naked onto the bed and falling into a deep sleep.

Juliette went to her office to file receipts and balance

her books, soon becoming immersed in the paperwork of her land as Axel slept her innocent hours away. As the sun dropped and left the windows of the office empty, Madame Gautier knocked and came in to tell Juliette that she could hear noises from Axel's room of a bath being run, and should she prepare dinner?

'Oh, the time has come too soon. Yes, yes, prepare the food. I think we shall eat on the veranda. Pleasantries are so much easier in the open air. I have no other guests tonight, so there will only be the two of us.'

Juliette crossed the hall, went into the drawing room and poured a drink. How long will she be? Will she need an extended toilette? Make-up? Ironing? Who knows?

Axel stood in front of the mirror and tried to imagine herself as others saw her, sighing as she failed. What to wear? What would be appropriate? The place seemed relaxed and easy-going. Perhaps she was over-dressed? She ripped off her jeans and sorted through her creased clothes. Nothing, I can't wear anything.

Juliette pulled gently at the sleeves of her silk blouse, straightened the seams of her stockings and poured another drink, as she wandered around the drawing room wishing she could go back to her office.

Axel crept down the stairs, unsure of where to go until she heard plates clattering in the kitchen. She felt her way down the dimly lit hall and found Madame Gautier, who looked at her t-shirt and jeans in amazement.

'Madame Guillot?' asked Axel in a cracked voice.

The cook beckoned and Axel followed her back down the hallway until they reached enormous double doors on which the cook rapped her knuckles. Hearing the rap, Juliette turned, steeling herself.

'Entrez!'

The door opened and Axel came in, closing the door behind her. Juliette stood unmoving and gazed at her guest, whose tall, rangy body stood awkwardly, whose face caught the last of the sun, whose big, bony hands were raised to shield her astonishing eyes. Collecting herself, Juliette crossed the room and opened her arms to kiss Axel, who had thrust her hand forward, and the two collided.

'Bonsoir, Mademoiselle Axel,' said Juliette and kissed her lightly on both cheeks.

'Um ... hello. I mean, hello Madame ... Guillot.' Axel withdrew her hand and shifted her weight from one foot to the other.

'No, no, you must call me Juliette,' she said, standing back. 'Would you like a drink? I expect you will want a gin and tonic.'

'No, thank you, I mean, yes. Do you have a beer?'

'A beer? Like English beer? Brown?'

'No, I'm sorry. I mean lager beer.'

'Yes, I think so.' Juliette rummaged in the cabinet and found one of the squat, dusty bottles which she emptied into a crystal glass. 'Voilà. Well, cheers.'

'Cheers.' Axel swallowed half her beer.

'Do sit down – or would you rather sit outside?'

'Outside would be nice.'

Axel was treated once more to a view of the estate as she settled into a chair. Looking up she realised her room was above the drawing room, facing south. 'Er, thank you for the room. I like it.'

'Good, good. Well, it is the best of all the rooms that are unoccupied. I thought you would like it.'

'Your English is very good.'

Juliette smiled at the bluntness of the remark and revised the image of Axel that she would carry around with her. 'Thank you, I have worked at it for a very long time. As, I believe, you will have to do with my own tortuous language.'

'Yes.' Axel stretched and looked out at the vines, searching for the river.

'There is a river down there at the foot of this valley, Axel. I only mention it because your mother told me that you are a very good swimmer and like to be near water.'

'I know. I swam there this afternoon.'

'This afternoon?'

'Yes.'

Juliette laughed as she thought of her conversation

with the cook, who now came out onto the veranda and laid plates of cold meat and poultry, bowls of salad, boards of cheese and baskets of bread on the table. As the cook poured the wine Juliette told her of Axel's swim. The two women looked over to the girl who stared still at the landscape. Juliette asked Madame Gautier to stock more beer and to chill bottles for the future. She turned back to her guest.

'So, Axel, how is your family? Or, rather, how is your mother? I have not seen her for a very long time.'

'She's doing very well. She's got nine shops now.'

'No, I mean how is she? I realise that she is doing well, she always will. How long is it now that her husband, your father, has been gone?' Juliette had realised that Axel had little time for social niceties, probably because she would not understand them.

'Nine years.' Axel broke a baguette and started meticulously to fill it with meat and salad.

'As long as that? I am amazed. It amazes me more that he left your mother to marry my sister. It shows a lack of taste surprising even in a man.'

For the first time since she had arrived Axel laughed aloud.

'And your brother, Byron, how is he?'

Axel chewed and swallowed. 'Alright I think. I don't see him much at the moment. He's still at school at Downside.'

'Downside? Is that one of the private schools?'

'Yes. Only they're called public schools, being anything but.'

'Oh, yes, I remember now. You have just finished your schooling I believe.'

'Mmmm.' Axel began to load her plate with salad.

'And you have done your Baccalauréat?'

'We call them 'A-levels'. Yes, last week.'

'And you have done well?'

Axel frowned and laid down her bread, still chewing. 'No, not very. I only did three subjects, but I wasn't very good at any of them. English, history and geography. A typical, middle-class girl's combination.' Axel forked a slice of cold duck. 'I've done well enough to go to university, I hope. Strange. You're the first person who's asked me. My mother just seems to hold her breath and hope that I won't fall asleep. This meal is delicious.'

Juliette realised that she had been holding her breath in much the same way, as she listened to Axel speak whole, if disjointed, sentences. 'At which university will you be studying?'

'Exeter. Doing English.'

'Why Exeter? Does it have a good English department?'

'No. Not really. It's near the sea,' said Axel with an air of stating the obvious.

'Oh, I see.'

Axel fell silent and concentrated on the food, slowly clearing plate after plate, as Juliette picked at a small salad.

'When will you be going to Exeter Axel?' asked Juliette when she found the silence too oppressive.

'A year in October. Could I have another beer please? I'm too thirsty for wine; although it's very nice.'

'It should be, it is fifty-nine of my own vines.'

'Oh, I'm sorry.'

'No matter. Help yourself to anything you would like.'

'Thank you.' Axel found some more beer and sat down again. 'Um, Juliette, there's something I'd like to say. About my being here. I realise that it's an imposition and I would never have asked. My mother suggested it and said that if I were left to my own devices I'd do nothing with my year off before going to Exeter. She was right as usual. If you would rather I left, I will.'

'Of course you will not. I need as many workers as I can find here. You are welcome to stay as long as you wish, although I believe your mother said you would be leaving in the first week of November.'

'That's right. To be home for my birthday. It's my eighteenth.'

'You are only seventeen?'

'Yes.'

'Mon dieu, you are very big for someone so young.'

'I know.'

'However, you may stay or leave when you wish. But please feel welcome to stay.'

'Thank you. Thank you for your hospitality.'

'It is not hospitality. You will be working for me.'

Axel blushed and shifted in her chair. 'Of course.'

'Have you ever worked before?'

'A little.'

'Doing what?'

'Hospital work.'

'C'est bien. That means you can get up early, which you will have to do. Obviously you are strong and healthy, which is another good thing. You will have to learn some French. Until September, the ban de vendanges, there is mainly maintenance work to be done, on machinery and buildings. If I ask you to scrub floors, whitewash walls, wash my car, can I assume you will do it?'

'Yes.' Axel was shocked by the change in Juliette from elegant, relaxed hostess to businesswoman; she had never noticed her mother's similar shift.

'Bon. You will work from seven in the morning until mid-day and from four until seven, six days a week. All except Sunday. Obviously this will be changed according to the weather and the hours of sunlight later in the year. I do not expect you to go to church on your free day,' Juliette said with a smile, but Axel was too shocked to notice. 'I will pay you two hundred francs a week, which may not sound like very much, but you will have your room and food provided. However, having now seen you eat I am not sure that this is a good arrangement.'

'But ... Juliette, you don't need to pay me. I'll be here in the sun, with the river. It's enough. I have some money.'

'Axel,' Juliette snapped, 'never work for nothing. It is worse than foolish, it is suicide. If you work, you are paid. C'est la vie. Do not sell yourself short as the English say. You will find that someone else will always do that for you. Do not be stupid.'

'I'm sorry.'

'You may, of course, ask me for a couple of days off

if you wish to go to Paris or Bordeaux or Toulouse, or perhaps to sleep. You may possibly be here for five months. I do not expect you to work the whole time.' Juliette poured a glass of wine and drank it. 'So – are we understood? I do not wish there to be any mistakes. You are Alexandria's daughter, I would like you to enjoy yourself. But we must understand one another.'

'Yes. I understand. Thank you. I'll work hard, I promise.'

Juliette offered her hand and Axel shook it, wondering what it was she would be doing for the next few months.

'Good, that is over. Now, Axel, would you like more beer? Yes? Help yourself. Please understand – if you are going to sweat blood for me, you might as well treat yourself to whatever you would like while you are here.' This time Axel caught the smile and returned it.

They sat on in the dying light, speaking of the district and the places to see, the family and the people they had in common, the vines and land on which the Guillots had built their fortune. Juliette, by now accustomed to Axel's silences and brief answers and revelling in the opportunity to talk to a stranger of these things, talked until her throaty voice cracked.

'Well, Axel,' she said finally, glancing at her watch, 'it is late. You must be up at six o'clock to have breakfast – in your case, half-past five perhaps, to manage all you will eat. Madame Gautier will knock at your door at six. I expect you in the yard at seven. So.' She stood and walked around the table to Axel. 'It has been a pleasure to meet you at last, having heard so much about you, mostly from my sister I must confess, and therefore mostly bad. I am glad my forebodings have been proved wrong. I know that Alexandria's daughter will be nothing if not a good worker.' A shadow flitted across Axel's eyes as she heard this, noted by Juliette. 'Alors, dors bien.' Again the two of them embraced awkwardly, before Juliette could perform the ritual kiss. Axel returned the gesture woodenly, bumping with her lips. She has never been touched, thought Juliette as she climbed the stairs.

The next morning Axel stumbled into the yard, blinded by the sunshine. She stood blinking and shivering, not knowing how cold it would be at that hour. She heard the churning and grinding of a tractor nearby and shielded her eyes to see it. Juliette drove through the gate and into the yard, urging on the old tractor in loud guttural French. She brought it to a shuddering halt in front of Axel and jumped down, gesturing to a worker to move it on.

'Bonjour Axel,' she shouted above the noise, wiping her hands on the dirty blue overalls she wore. 'You slept well?'

'Bonjour Madame ... Juliette. Yes, thank you.' Axel could barely recognise the woman of the night before.

'You have no ... what is the word? Woolly? No – jumper. You have no jumper? You must be cold. Wait.' Juliette crossed to a dark out-house and reappeared holding a filthy, tattered sweatshirt. 'Voilà. It is one of Hugo's, but he is already out in the fields and will not use it.' Axel pulled on the stiffened shirt, not minding its musty smell. 'Do you drive Axel?'

'Yes, not for long though.'

'Have you driven a tractor?'

'No, never. Is it difficult?' Axel stamped her feet to start her hot blood moving.

'It is different. No matter, I shall ask Henri to teach you later. Follow me, I will show you the estate and tell you the things you will need to know.' Juliette re-tied her headscarf and set off quickly, swinging round the back of the house and to its west side.

'Down there, by the river, you see a small wooden hut?' asked Juliette pointing down the gentle slope.

'Yes.'

'In there you will find some scythes which we use to cut back the *haies* – the small hedges – along the river. Up there, next to the office window you see a box; that contains keys to unlock that hut and that brick out-house over there in which you will find some diesel and oil for the tractors should you run out in the fields. That is opened by the yellow key. Down there is Field 13 — I do not know why it is called that — next to the small orchard, which you can only reach by cutting through the plot ...' And so on and on and on.

The two of them walked for miles around the estate, Juliette occasionally stopping to talk to other workers, laughing with them and introducing Axel. As the morning sun rose higher so Axel began to sweat. She took off the sweatshirt and hung it around her neck, then tied it round her waist. Soon she was dipping her head under the taps in the corners of fields as Juliette talked to someone, frustrated she could not drink the water. Juliette's voice went on, her finger pointing to some now-shimmering speck in the distance, Axel noting neither. Three hours after they had left the yard they returned to it, Axel panting with thirst and soaking wet. Juliette's brown skin was dry and her hair, when she shook it loose from the scarf, was as it had been the night before.

'Excuse me,' Axel croaked, 'I have to have something to drink.' She ran into the dim, shuttered kitchen and groped for the bottle of water on the table and, finding it, gulped down half its contents, unaware of it splashing down her face and throat.

'Sorry,' she mumbled, outside once more.

'You will become accustomed to it.' Juliette lit a cigarette and stopped a passing man to ask him to find Henri.

'I'm afraid I can't remember much of what you said.'

'I know. However, you will be surprised by how much you remember when necessary. Ah, Henri.' She turned to a weasel-faced young man and introduced the two. 'Excuse me, Axel, I must speak French.' Soon she turned back again. 'Axel, I want you to go with Henri to Field 13 and fill the trailer as he'll show you. He'll drive alongside you along the rows. Later he will show you how to drive, although you will have to practice, of course. A bientôt.' Juliette turned to go but stopped in the doorway. 'One piece of advice. Do things slowly. It is hot. Do not race.'

Axel lay down on her bed slowly that afternoon, having wolfed down three bowls of chicken and noodles. Gingerly she touched her shoulders, her burning skin prickling under her fingers. Fingers which were bloodied at the tips and hands beginning to blister at the palm. It seemed no sooner had she fallen asleep than Madame Gautier was hammering at her door, calling her to the afternoon shift. As she ground the gears of the tractor, stalling in every corner of the field, unable to understand and so act on Henri's bawled instructions, she smiled to herself, remembering her vision of afternoons spent swimming in the limpid waters of the river and sprawling on its banks. She laughed aloud, annoying Henri, as she remembered her offer to work for nothing.

'Bugger!' she shouted, trying to drag the gearstick down, bouncing on the steel seat.

It seemed an age had passed before Henri waved to her and pointed to his wrist and then at the house. She climbed down painfully and balanced on the back of the tractor, clinging to Henri's sloping, jutting-bone shoulders as he drove her to the house.

'Merci,' she croaked when he left her by the kitchen door.

'A bientôt!' he called back, grinning evilly.

'Bloody hope not,' she muttered, walking stiffly into the kitchen.

Madame Gautier let loose a stream of solicitude before remembering Axel could not understand a word, shrugged and turned away. Axel coughed to recapture her attention.

'Lait?' she said hopefully when the other turned round.

'Mais, bien sûr. Là-bas'. She pointed to the fridge. Axel looked and found a large jug which she put on the scarred wooden table. Fetching a glass she sat down and winced.

Juliette came in, dressed in billowing cotton, holding a sheaf of papers. Seeing Axel she stopped in mid-question to the cook and sat down opposite.

'How has your day been?'
'Fine.'
'How is the driving?'
'Fine.'
Juliette looked at her more closely. 'But your face

and shoulders are burnt. They look very painful.' She stretched out her hand to lay her fingertips on Axel's russet forehead. Axel fought down the desire to brush them away. 'This is no good. I forget that you do not see the sun in England. Have you a hat?'

'No.' Axel drank more milk, leaving a thin white moustache on her reddening face.

'Alors, we must find one. Ah, I think I have an old one you can wear tomorrow. Also you must wear a shirt with sleeves tomorrow or you will blister. Now you must bath and put lots of camomile on your skin.' Juliette asked Madame Gautier to fetch a bottle. 'I shall be dining at eight o'clock if you would like to join me?'

Axel looked desperately at the older woman, knowing she could not refuse, but thinking only of the white cotton sheets and cold grey light in her room, and the slats of light on the white walls. 'Yes, of course. Thank you. I'd better wash.' She pushed herself up and left, not seeing Juliette's appraising look.

When Axel fell asleep as she cut a peach, Juliette gently woke her and told her to go to bed.

'Do not worry too much, Axel,' she said, as the other stared at the room, trying to remember where she was, 'it is only two more days until Sunday.'

Axel slept until mid-day that Sunday, waking only to eat and then returning to her bed, ignoring the winking eyes of the river as it glistened through the distant trees. She woke again at four and drew a deep hot bath. Lying in the water she looked at her body for the first time since she had arrived. Her toenails were black, her feet white. Her ankles were scratched and small scabs were scattered across them where she had been bitten. Her knees and thighs were bruised where she had rested slabs of stone before lifting them. Her stomach and back were red where the sun had touched them as she bent to pick things up and then lift them high. Her shoulders had peeled to reveal pinker skin. Her forearms were scratched and bruised, her hands a mass of blisters. Having towelled herself she looked in the small mirror and found her neck was red, a red which stopped suddenly and became white. Her nose, too, had peeled. Across her forehead there was a line where Juliette's old trilby – a relic from her more liquid, fashion-conscious days – had rested. To cheer herself she looked into her eyes only to find that even these looked different.

Lying naked on her bed she drank some beer, smoked cigarettes and tried to learn how to conjugate the verbs être, manger and avoir, but soon became bored. Throwing the book to the floor she turned and stared at the ceiling, knowing Madame Gautier would not be knocking at her door. As she stretched her stiff limbs, feeling the oils she had smoothed on herself sinking into her parched skin, she became aware that she was wondering what it would be like if someone else were there on the bed with her. Axel blushed and got up to dress carefully, easing her clothes over her stinging flesh. Without thinking she picked up the trilby and pulled it over her eyes. As she opened the door she looked back into the room, saw the light slatting the far wall, saw the jumbled pile of clothes at the foot of the bed, saw the small empty bottles of beer, saw the full ashtray, saw the rumpled sheets, and again she wondered about the absent body.

In the late afternoon sun she walked the dusty roads around Sainte-Croix-de-Mont, walked for miles and yet never lost sight of Juliette's awesome house. She saw few people – a woman shaking a sheet out of a first-floor window; a child poking a lethargic dog with a stick; a couple eating in their garden; an old woman in her Sunday clothes setting off for church. Cars passed her, young men hooting and waving. She felt her muscles loosening, her legs and buttocks unbunching as she walked. She realised she had not thought of her mother or brother or London at all and, having realised this, did not then know what to think of them. All the time she had been away she had talked to no one except Juliette; for Axel this was enough, she rarely talked to more than one person. Perhaps it was this that enabled her to be immediately content in this foreign place.

2

Juliette watched Axel closely during her first two weeks, watched to make sure she was not unhappy. She knew this was a difficult task, having realised that Axel would show misery in a way few others would share. Watching her, she saw Axel change, as her skin darkened to golden brown; as her body became firmer, more muscled, stronger; as her hair lightened to ash-blonde. But Juliette saw no unhappiness – indeed, Axel laughed more each day as she understood a little more of what was being said around her. Juliette would watch Axel working, dressed in tattered shorts, a vest and the ubiquitous trilby, and noticed the careful strength of her movements, the speed with which she learned from others the most economical way of lifting, shovelling, carrying, pulling, digging. Juliette was irked that the earth would, inevitably, lose such a caring worker, feeling that Axel would be happier if she never strayed from it.

Each evening the two of them would meet over dinner and their talk became more and more often concerned with the estate as Axel learned. Each evening Juliette would notice a change in the other – a new scar, a deeper tan, another freckle, the movement of a previously unused muscle – and so became more aware of her own more static state. As Juliette worried less over Axel's happiness, so they relaxed in each other's company; talk became sparse between these two people who lived their lives alone. Juliette would read trade journals and reports as Axel ate, always slowly and appreciatively, remarking on various dishes. Madame Gautier wondered at herself for having judged Axel so harshly.

A month passed, in which Juliette came, oddly, to respect Axel, despite the disparity in their ages and life-styles. She respected Axel for her evident ethical code, for her strength, her ability to make things work, her epicurean delight in food and wine, and most of all for her literalness. She came to enjoy Axel's silent company.

On one of these indigo nights in August, Madame

Gautier came out to say that there was a telephone call for Axel, she could take it in the hall if she wished. Axel looked startled.

'A phone call? Who is it?'

Madame Gautier shrugged and left.

'Who can it be?' Axel frowned as she stood to light a cigarette.

'Why not go to find out?' Juliette looked down again at her magazine.

In the hall Madame Gautier handed a heavy old telephone to her and disappeared.

'Hello?' Axel shivered in her shorts.

'Hello? Axel?' The voice was faint and scratchy.

'Hello? Who is it?'

'You don't recognise your own mother? After only one month?'

'God! Mother! How are you?' Axel shouted, her voice echoing in the deep, empty hall.

'I called to ask you the same. A letter, Axel, would have been welcome.'

'Oh, I'm sorry.' Axel blew out a plume of smoke as she tried to remember how to talk to someone who was not Juliette.

'I was worried for a while. Then I thought that if anything had happened I would have had a postcard from Rio.' Alexandria, too, was having trouble trying to work out how to talk to her eldest and most-loved child; the child she knew would slip away as easily as the fish that same child loved, with a flash-silver hardly disturbing the water, so swiftly it would seem never to have happened.

'I'll write this week.'

'Don't bother, you write terrible letters.'

In the silence that followed each felt the other's heart beating from within, felt the clamour of unsaid things.

'Well, Axel, aren't you going to ask the obvious?'

'What?' Axel searched her mind for things she could say, but found nothing except pictures of long, hot days and contentment.

'Your exam results came today.'

'Oh my God, I'd forgotten about that.'

On the other end of the line Alexandria smiled at this coolness, thinking it was assumed. 'You've done well enough. Enough to go to Exeter. You could have done better. But I don't suppose I'm telling you anything that you don't know already.'

'No, I suppose you're not.'

'So, are you having a good time?'

'Have you ever been here mother?'

'No. I haven't. I've only heard Juliette's descriptions. It sounds wonderful.'

'If you'd been here you'd know I was having a good time. It *is* wonderful. There's a river.'

Alexandria closed her eyes, wishing she had been to Sainte-Croix-de-Mont, indeed, wishing herself there. 'So, you're happy.'

'Yes. Very.'

'Good. Let me know when you're coming home.' Alexandria tried to keep the bitterness from her voice but Axel tasted it – like a flake of pure tobacco on the tip of her tongue.

'I'm coming home in November – if not before. You know that.'

'Yes, well, let me know. I'll meet you from the plane. ... Axel?'

'Yes?'

'Look after yourself ... I ...'

'What? The line's fuzzy.'

'I look forward to November. Call me.' Alexandria, the newly styled cynic, threw the telephone down and walked quickly to her library. Why? Why couldn't she say 'I love you' to her own daughter? She lashed out feebly at a pile of books on the table. Had Michael gagged her as well as leaving her?

Axel returned to the veranda, silenced by a rush of homesickness.

'Who was it, if I might ask?' Juliette poured Axel some wine.

'My mother.'

'Ah! How is she?'

'Alright I suppose. She didn't say much.' Axel frowned and swallowed loudly.

'She has never been – what do you say – verbose.'

18

'No. Well, perhaps she was.'

'What do you mean?'

'I don't know. She's changed a lot. Since she was divorced. I can remember her being very different.'

'Yes, I know what you mean. She has become quieter.'

'When did you last see her?'

'Oh, I'm not sure. Perhaps a year ago.'

'Then you know what I mean.'

As they sat sipping the wine Juliette became aware for the first time of Axel's slowly turning motor, a tiny vibration she could feel through the room. It was an awareness that never again left her – of a motor triggered by anger.

'Axel.' The other did not hear. 'Axel.' This time she looked up and their eyes locked. 'Do you see your father at all?'

'Sometimes.'

'But you do not like him, do you?'

'No – I fucking hate him!' Axel had jumped to her feet, toppling the chair. 'I only go because Byron goes now and then,' she said in a calmer voice as she righted the chair. 'I feel I have to go to protect Byron. I think my father's scared of me. Doesn't that sound silly?' And the motor slowly ground down to an imperceptible murmur again.

That night Axel slept fitfully for the first time since she had arrived at Juliette's. The faces of her family swam in front of her ever-reddening eyes as she turned and turned again on the hard bed. She saw the gun-metal of dawn through the shutters and struggled her way out of the damp, rucked sheets, opened the window and stared out at the fecund land around her. Axel's brick-brown skin puckered in the cold and her hands shook as she lit a cigarette. To displace the kaleidoscope of misgivings whirling in her untutored mind she tried to imagine the Garonne passing silently below her. But as she pictured its unceasing flow, the faces of her mother, her father, Byron and Juliette reappeared, flowering under the sheen of water, as if smiling but drowning. Axel dropped the butt and crushed it with her hardened foot. She went into the bathroom, filled the sink with cold water and plunged her head in until her ears were covered but still the drumming hammered. So she stayed until her breath failed her, then flung her head away from the sink, spattering the floor and bath behind her as her hair spun in an arc. As the bedroom filled with warmth, she lay unsleeping on the saturated flattened pillows, nursing herself with strong arms.

3

The next morning Axel tried to bat the needles from her eyes as Juliette directed her to trim the hedges of the fields, telling her to fetch a short-sickle from the shed, showing her the fields to work in with a sweep of her arm. Juliette had noticed the fine-spun deltas of blood that ran from Axel's shocking irises but hardened her heart to them. The yard was full of men and women in stained work-clothes, who nodded to Axel as she pulled her hat on and left alone. The day before a pipe had burst somewhere in the irrigation system and the workers and farmhands had been gathered together so Juliette could allocate them to check the taps and outlets in every field, orchard and vinery. Between them, Juliette and the overseer distributed the workers in less than an hour.

Axel had collected the sickle and one thick rubber glove and walked to the start of the two-kilometre stretch of field boundaries she was to tidy. Slipping the glove onto her left hand she started to work, hacking at the tough roots of old vines which had been woven together many years before but which had become a tangled, overgrown mess. With her gloved hand she pulled at the chalk and old fencing. Now her back was strong and supple, her wrists had thickened; she no longer felt her muscles and joints bunching and creaking. As she crept along a stretch of rotten, weed-infested *haies* she missed the sound of tractors and scratching of hoes; all she could hear was the voice of the overseer as he meandered along distant roads in a car, bawling instructions through a megaphone. Axel pulled off the glove with her teeth as she searched for her cigarettes, smiling when she saw her puckered, sweaty hand revealed, slightly paler than the right as it was more often in a glove. Squatting down to avoid the sun she wondered about the night-fright she had had, bouncing gently on her heels, trying to forget it as she looked at the burgeoning earth around her.

A scream, high-pitched but stunted by the hot dead air, reached Axel and she jumped to her feet, quivering. Again the scream screeched through the mid-day heat waves and she began to run towards it, vaulting gates, climbing over walls and fighting through tangles of vine stems, responding to the animal-shout of a man in pain. She did not notice the cuts blossoming on her body as she covered the ground between her and the source of the scream; did not notice the gash in her softened left hand, cut by a thrusting chunk of limestone; did not notice the rasping of her closing throat as she answered a bellow of agony. Scrambling over the ditch bordering Field 13 she knew she was near. Shading her eyes with a trembling hand she picked out a man lying in the far corner. Running towards him she realised what had happened: an open-topped, steel tank had broken away from its supports and fallen across the man's legs. Normally empty, it had been filled by the overflow from the burst pipe. The tank had only tipped a little, cushioning its fall on the fleshy shins of the man who had assumed it was empty.

Axel, her momentum unbroken, hurled herself at the tank with her shoulder and rebounded, the tank unmoved. Again the man let out a baying sound. Picking herself up Axel planted her feet squarely and heaved at the metal cube, her palms aching as they were cut by flakes of rust, her shouts of frustration mixing with the howls of the injured man. Falling back from the immobile tank she realised it was the water weighing it down. Desperately she looked around for something to puncture the metal skin. Propped against a post she saw a spade glinting in the dazzling light. As Axel raised the spade high above her head she looked at the man's face for the first time and saw a pair of uncomprehending eyes and a twisted mouth silenced by the path of the spade which sliced down and struck the metal just above his legs. Again and again she struck, using a corner of the spade, forcing the metal ever inward, punching it until a hole appeared. Still she hammered at it until the fine spray became a stream and the water began to pour away. Throwing the spade down on the now-soaking earth she braced herself once more and pushed again, grunting with effort. Suddenly other hands were next to hers and the tank toppled over, freeing the man beneath it. Axel was surrounded by other people as she bent over, hands on her knees, trying to slow the thudding in her chest. The workers shouted instructions to each other, confusion taking the upper hand until Juliette appeared.

'Qu'est qu'il se passe?' she shouted, running down the straight lines of vines.

A worker turned and, pointing to Axel and the tank, began to explain.

'Axel! What happened?' Juliette stooped to look into Axel's face. Axel explained in short, breathless sentences, trying not to look at the injured man's bloody legs.

'How did you move the tank?' asked Juliette as Axel straightened.

'I made a hole in it. To let the water out.'

'You made a hole in the tank? There is a hole in the tank?' Juliette pushed through the group of workers to see the damage. Pointing to the jagged, much-dented tear, she asked, 'You did this?'

'Yes.'

'And how do you suppose it will be mended? And what about these vines?' Juliette was standing face to face with Axel once more, the others standing back, watching silently, waiting for an ambulance.

'What about them?' Axel's motor slowly ground, ball in socket.

'They are wet, saturated. It is only fourteen more days until the vintage. They are useless.' Juliette's face was taut and contorted, her hair flying as she jerked her eyes from the toppled tank to the now useless earth.

'If I hadn't done it, I couldn't have moved the tank,' Axel said slowly, enunciating every word as her gears changed.

'But if you had waited a moment – no more – we could all have moved it. Now it must be replaced and the vines are ruined.'

Around the two of them the others stood unmoving, still silent, feeling the air for emotion as they could not understand the language of this electric exchange. Axel was shocked, being still young enough to imagine Juliette to be flawless.

'I didn't know how long anyone would be.'

'You did not think.'

'You don't care.'

Juliette looked up into Axel's eyes and felt fearful. She tried to outstare Axel, tried to force Axel's eyes to shift: but then she felt the pulse of the motor growing; imagined the force that had punched a hole in a steel tank; became aware of the strength of Axel's conviction. Juliette glanced at the shattered steel, at the bruised, bloody legs of the prostrate man and hissed: 'Maybe. I suppose you were not to know how long we would be.'

'No.'

Axel's eyes had not moved from Juliette's. The older woman felt increasingly uneasy. She noticed the chalky, dusty earth becoming wet and slimy. She turned and shouted at another woman to turn off the mains in the next field. Hearing the ambulance, she sent a couple of workers to meet and direct the stretcher-bearers. The injured man groaned, shaking everyone back to the present. Juliette barked orders, short and hoarse, irritated to see all these man hours wasted, telling the gathered workers to go to find the supervisor in the yard and get their new work. As they filed away, glancing at Juliette, surprised by her brusqueness, the two men with the stretcher appeared.

'Over here!' shouted Juliette. 'You may go Axel. Finish your work.'

The injured man gestured to Axel, muttering strange sounds, dulled and rounded. He beckoned her over.

'Merci,' he croaked as she bent over him. Axel smiled and rubbed his shoulder. 'Merci.'

The ambulance men arrived to lay him on the stretcher and Axel stood and moved aside.

'Who is he?' she asked Juliette.

'Hugo.'

'Will he be alright?'

'I hope so. He's one of my best workers.' Juliette was chewing the ball of her thumb, assessing the torn skin and crooked angles of Hugo's legs.

'He seems very shocked. I mean, he's not talking clearly.'

'Of course he is not. He is from the hospital, the ... l'asile. He is ... I do not know ... l'aliéné. He is l'aliéné,' said Juliette, tapping her temple.

'He's mad?'

'Non. Pas cinglé. A little of him is cracked, broken. Not missing. However, it is a very little. He works well.'

'You mean he comes from a loony bin?'

'Loony bin?'

'You know, an ... an ... ah, shit, what's the word? An asylum, that's it. An asylum?'

'Oui, oui. L'asile. The asylum. In Cadillac.'

Work was forgotten as Axel turned to watch Hugo being lifted.

'But he's so handsome,' she whispered.

'Yes he is.'

The two of them watched Hugo being carried away, Axel waving as she tried to sift her emotions.

'Merci!' Hugo bawled, his voice still muffled, as he was carried away.

As the sun reached its peak Juliette and Axel found themselves left alone in Field 13, water still seeping through the ground beneath them. The sunlight reflected up into their faces in such a way that there was nowhere to hide.

'I didn't realise.' Axel swallowed with difficulty and stared at a vine leaf.

'Would it have made any difference?'

'No, no. Of course not.' Axel picked up her glove which she had brought with her, not knowing why. 'I don't think you're right,' she said, straightening.

Juliette — who had lived through bombings, seen random death, suffered celibacy, loneliness; who had directed hundreds of workers; who had taken a dead vineyard and breathed life into it; who had refused offer after offer as she slipped from beds in the early morning — did not know how to respond, how to quell this foreigner on her land.

'Go back to work. We do not have anything to say to each other now.' With that, Juliette offered a cigarette to Axel, held the packet out across the empty space between them in an attempt to bridge it. Axel looked at the cigarette, then at Juliette's tanned, trembling hand. Her eyes moved slowly up Juliette's arm, across her bare shoulders sheened with sweat, down past the crumpled vest and shorts to the bare feet. Axel wanted ... wanted what? Imagined what? She looked quickly into Juliette's eyes and was for a moment terrified, hoping she did not recognise what she found there. As she turned away to walk back to the *haies* she noticed the cigarette trembling still.

Once more, as she watched Axel stride through the regiments of vines, watched her vault a fence, watched her pause now and again to feel a leaf, to pick a grape, to rake the earth with her fingers and throw the larger stones into the ditch, Juliette wished Axel would stay, if not at Sainte-Croix-de-Mont, then somewhere where she would do these things. For Juliette knew that Axel would only be happy on the land, by the water, walking into the sea. And as Axel blurred into the sun, becoming invisible, Juliette tried to imagine her walking pavements, rising in lifts, falling on escalators, punching a keyboard, sitting in a purring, stationary car, putting bottles of detergent in a shopping trolley, buying a pressure cooker, and she could not. Shielding her eyes she searched for Axel, but had lost her in the heart of the sun.

4

Axel woke the next morning and saw sunlight striping her bed, a lattice-work of burnished, polished blue at her windows. She threw on some clothes and went down to breakfast, aching to drive to the sea – or so she thought the ache would be eased. She felt restless and went to find Juliette, who was in the kitchen discussing with Madame Gautier what should be bought on the next trip to the hypermarket on the outskirts of Bordeaux. Seeing Axel she waved her to sit down as she wrote a list of the things the cook called out. Axel poured herself some water and waited, watching Juliette. The minutes passed and still Juliette ignored her. Axel could feel her motor spinning, anxiety building. She slipped out of the room and out into the vineyard. She wished she was stripped, sweating, moving, moving. She walked to Field 13 and there, in its corner, was the tank, tilting crazily. Walking on to the river she sat on its banks, throwing stones into the rushing waters, but the river did not calm her, its churning only echoing her own. And as she sat, the feeling that was the most irksome, almost tangible, floated into her spinning guts and she smiled. She walked back to the house and asked Juliette if she could borrow a car to go into Bordeaux.

'Of course, take mine, it is the most comfortable.'

'If you want, I could go to the hypermarket and get the stuff you need,' said Axel, picking up the list on the kitchen table.

'No, there is too much for you to get on your own, someone would have to go with you. Although ... I suppose, yes, there are a few things we need. Here, take this short list and if you pass somewhere that is right, then get them. It is mainly frozen food and beer.' Juliette was having difficulty looking at Axel, was trying to avoid the girl's ceaseless stare. 'Also you will need some money. Here, take this.' Juliette rummaged in her bag and found a wad of notes, which she held out to Axel and then put quickly on the table.

'I'll buy some of it. I should contribute something to the household.' Axel almost snatched the list and car keys from Juliette's hand. 'Thanks. I'm not sure when I'll be back.' As Axel left the room Juliette relaxed visibly. She crossed to the window and watched Axel get into the car and drive off, waving vaguely as the car disappeared around the side of the house.

It was three in the morning when Axel woke from her shallow sleep and realised that it was the silence which had fallen piece by piece into the space around her which had dragged her from her dreams. Her eyes focused on the unfamiliar play of light and shade on one wall and the ceiling. The spines of the shutters of the hotel window were broken and the street lights shone through, lighting the room with a dim, neon flush. In her mind she replayed the evening she had spent in Bordeaux.

She had driven Juliette's Peugeot to its limits along the péage to the city. The exhilaration of being alone in a car had lifted her from her fitful depression. The speed of the car and her awareness of the possibilities of the evening had lifted her further. She felt truly free. She had taken the Mérignac road around the city and stopped to buy the provisions Juliette had listed. Then, with the car loaded, she had driven back to the centre of Bordeaux.

At first she drove round and round, watching people as they milled around the streets, catching buses, shrugging into coats outside restaurants, talking to drivers of cars through open passenger windows, sitting outside bars gesticulating and shouting. To Axel, who had been in the country for weeks seeing no one, the activity seemed extraordinary, almost orchestrated. She drove away from the centre, towards the train station, looking for a bar the name of which she dimly remembered. She drove down Cours Victor Hugo three times before she saw the flickering neon sign dangling over a door leading to a basement. She had parked and locked the car, with a twinge of guilt as it gleamed in the light of the seedy back-street, then walked back to the bar. As she went in the other people there stopped talking for a moment to eye her up and down and then turned back to their drinks. She smiled as she ordered a beer, knowing she had found what she wanted.

The walk from the bar to the hotel near the station had taken them through cobbled, one-lane streets full of drunks and fresh-faced innocents newly arrived on the late train from Paris. She had an image of Prufrock and his oyster shells as she savoured the smells and sounds of her illicit walk. The lateness of the hour, the intensity of the faces of the barflies, the boarded windows of warehouses – all these increased her sense of being outlawed.

Axel lay watching the lights flicker on the ceiling for a few moments more, letting the scenes playing in her mind's eye flicker and die, then she eased herself from the bed, careful not to disturb the other's even breathing. Once in the small bathroom she turned on the light and washed herself in the dribble of cold water coming from the shower. Towelling herself dry she felt that contradiction that follows sex: of being firm, yet relaxed; her body feeling tauter yet looser. She padded out, back to the bedroom, and dressed in the darkness. Leaning over the bed she looked at the clock: half-past three. She would be back at Juliette's by five.

'What time is it?' mumbled the woman curled under the covers, her voice slurred with tiredness.

'Half-three.'

'Uh.' The woman turned and pulled the pillow closer.

'I have to go now.'

'O.K.'

'I'll pay for the room when I leave.'

'Thanks.'

Leaning over the woman, Axel knew she should just leave now, but she disliked doing that – leaving without a backward glance.

'Um ...' What was her name? Katherine? Katrina? Kathy? 'Um ... Katalin?'

'Mmmmm?'

'Thank you, it was a good evening. Sleep well.' Axel patted the sheet-shrouded shoulder clumsily and flinched as it shrugged her off. She left, closing the door quietly.

The walk back to the car refreshed her, the coldness of the night air chilling her wrists and forehead. As she walked she thought how in control she felt – invincible, energy-filled. She thought of this time of the morning as the real dawn, the time at which the old day ends and another begins. Only people are interested in time, only they care about the twelve chimes of midnight. Alley cats slink through this time, through the curtain chink of the new day, smiling and preening. How many times will I slink from room to room, from door to door, from car to car? With that same alley-cat grin? Now, as she walked, she could see the last of the night people mingling with the market-stall holders, the fishmongers, the truck men delivering the first milk and newspapers, yawning taxi drivers, railwaymen ambling to the station. The night people melted away, trickled down alleys, turned swiftly into doorways.

Axel whistled tunelessly as she reached the car, only then remembering the frozen food in the boot. She threw open the boot and prodded the boxes and packets to find they were soft. On an impulse she slammed the boot shut and ran back the way she had come. Soon she saw what she was looking for – an old, grey, square-nosed Citröen van ramming its way over a pavement. As it snagged on a loose dustbin, she caught up with it and rapped the driver's window with her knuckles. She motioned to him to open the door.

'Wait!' she cried as he gunned the motor and tried to free the van. Realising he would have to move the bin he stepped out, cursing, and walked to the back of the van. He was wearing the faded blue cotton overalls and jacket of all workmen. His hair was white where it escaped from his cap.

'Excuse me,' Axel said, putting a hand on his arm, 'are you a fishmonger?'

'Yes,' he grunted, turning away to pull at the bin trapped in a wheelarch.

'Have you just come from Arcachon?'

'Yes.' He pulled out a bent cigarette from the top pocket of his jacket and straightened it, staring at Axel.

'How much have you got?'

'How much what?' He lit the cigarette and left it dangling from his purple lower lip.

'How much fish?'

'How much fish? Lots of it. I'm a fishmonger,' he said, looking away and edging past Axel.

'Can I see it?'

'See it? You want to see my fish?' He looked back at her more closely. She wasn't drunk or high – why did she want to see his fish? By the light of the street lamps he could see she was tall, beautiful and alone. There was something about her face that unsettled him, something he couldn't work out. It was too dark to put names to the different colours of Axel's eyes. He shuffled nearer, intrigued by her. She wasn't French. Why was this fearless, foreign woman singing to him about fish in the light of dawn? 'Why?' he asked eventually, moving even closer, his boots scraping on the kerb.

'Are they on ice? The fish?' She had not moved.

'Yes.' Stranger still.

'I want to buy everything you've got – and I'll take the ice for nothing.'

'What?' He stepped back. 'Everything I have? I am a fisherman not a shopkeeper. Do you know how much I have? Look!' He threw open the door to the van, opened a large insulated box in the back, which had two doors, like the doors to a cellar. 'Look! Pounds of fish, mussels, crabs, crayfish. See? Even squid!' He grew excited, waving at the cold, metallic skins and shells stacked in waxy cardboard boxes. He felt odd, confused. There was something about this woman that made him know she was serious.

'I can't see anything properly – have you got a light in here?' Axel could only make out shapes and cold colours, glints of basalt and mica amidst the snowfield of crushed ice.

'Yes, yes, I have a light – wait!' He ran round the

cabin of the van and switched on the light for the rear. Axel was surprised – there was a lot of fish, far more than she had imagined. She felt the old man at her shoulder, peering at his own produce. 'You want to buy all that?'

'Wait, I want to look at it.' She selected fish at random, holding them, testing their stiffness on her flat palm; she smelled the squid, squashing the flesh to see how much water ran out; she flicked a crab with hr fingers and flinched when it moved; she hauled a tunny fish out, out over the other fish, and felt its lacquer-like finish, squeezed its gut to check its firmness, she looked in the buckets of mussels and saw bubbles rising.

'How much for the lot?'

'You want to buy it all?'

'Well ... I don't really want the mussels. Maybe you could keep them?'

'Merde!' He spat on the road. 'I can't stand them.'

'O.K., but they'll have to go in boxes – I can't take them in buckets.'

'That's not so difficult.'

'So – how much?'

They turned to face each other in the dim light from the van. Axel felt she was on stage: the doors of the van the wings, the fish the audience.

'Well,' he shrugged, 'how much will you pay?'

'You tell me how much you'd get for them in the market and I'll add to it.'

'I couldn't tell you exactly – you know – it changes every day. Up and down, up and down.' The man moved his hands to illustrate his point.

'Tell me roughly how much.'

'Wait ... I must think.' He lit another cigarette from the stub of the first. Both of them looked into the van, their breaths mingling, misting as it drifted in. Both weighed the fish and shellfish in their minds, calculating, calculating.

'I've brought it all the way fron Arcachon ...' he said.

'And you can be back there by six. You get the day to yourself.'

'Only if you take the mussels too.'

'Yes, I've said I'll have them.'

'I work for myself, I don't have any other way of making money. It's a small business.'

'It's a long day.'

'Yes, yes.'

Again they stood in silence. Axel asked for a cigarette, which he lit for her.

'Three thousand francs,' he said suddenly, straightening.

'Two thousand – it's mostly tunny fish in weight and they're all head and shoulders, not much flesh.'

Silence fell once more.

'Ah, yes, maybe, but the crayfish are big today, very meaty.'

'True. Two thousand two hundred.'

They fell back against their respective doors. She knew two thousand two hundred was enough, that it would please him, but he was used to the cries and cajoling and bartering of the market.

'Look,' she said, shivering a little, 'I've got two thousand two hundred francs in cash, here, now, and very little more. You could be in Arcachon by six with the money. It's enough.'

He watched her as she spoke, knowing that every moment he wasted was money wasted at the market. He also knew that at least six hundred francs was clear profit – not bad for a morning's work.

'O.K. – two thousand two hundred. It's robbery, but it saves time. My name is Réné Debussy.' He held out his calloused hand.

'Mademoiselle Frechotte,' she said. They smiled broadly at one another.

Axel backed the Peugeot down the street until the boot was nearly touching the van and she and the old man unloaded the fish. They poured the ice over the soft boxes, Axel hoping to save the food at the bottom. Then they lowered the back seat, laying the boxes of fish along the back, in the foot wells, on the passenger's seat, jamming them in every space they could find. They were sweating when they finished, despite the cold and their frozen hands which creaked when they stretched their fingers. Crushed ice was scattered around them, glinting on the road. The sky was beginning to lighten, its leaden weight of darkness rolling away.

'You have so much fish!' the old man yelped, delighted by the picture he had helped to create. 'You will be eating bouillabaisse for months!' He laughed, pointing at the shining car, filled normally with the lingering scent of Juliette's perfume. Axel blew on her fingers, trying to make them move, then she too looked at the car, imagining Juliette's face if she could see it, and started to laugh. Fucking crazy, she thought, what am I doing? She pulled the money out of a hidden pocket in her jacket and started to count out twenty-two hundred franc notes into the outstretched yellowed hand. She watched the man's bloodshot eyes flick from her hand to his own, his glee growing. On impulse she added another note. 'For the ice and your help.'

Their parting was prolonged by Monsieur Debussy giving her his address, his eyes twinkling as he told her to contact him if she needed more fish, and to visit when she was in Arcachon. She could feel his delight over the episode as she shook his hand before getting in the car. She imagined him waking his wife to tell her, recounting the story over breakfast, to his friends in bars, to his family, to strangers. She imagined him laughing whenever he passed the spot on his way to the market. As she drove off she waved through the open window until she turned a corner.

The drive back to Juliette's was long, cold and silent. Axel kept glancing at the stiff heads and glassy eyes of the fish near her and wishing she were home. The windows were open to keep the air fresh and to keep her awake. The exhilaration of the evening was passing, yet still she didn't feel tired. The swishing sound of passing trees became rhythmic, dulling. Her mouth and eyes were dry and prickly, her skin numb, making the steering wheel difficult to hold. Axel's mind pounded as relentlessly as the tires on the road.

And as she drove nearer to Juliette, passing through miles of dark, enclosed country, thick with woods

and vineyards, towards Sainte-Croix-de-Mont, where
Juliette murmured through her tangled dreams, Axel
thought of that lonely woman in her château. Her
mind slipped easily from the woman she had left in
the hotel room to Juliette's bedroom, where she now
knew she wanted to be. But she could not wish that –
should not wish that. She reached out and turned on
the radio to silence herself but found only static. She
turned the dial savagely and switched it off. What to
do? What was it she had seen in Juliette's eyes the day
before, standing in a muddy field? Was she mistaken?
What to do?

Once back at Juliette's she called to the dogs from
the car, letting them know who she was before getting
out. In the greying light the fish lost their jet and silver
colours, became mundane as she hauled box after box
into the huge freezer room and piled them into one
chest after another. She emerged from the barn to see
the clouds on the horizon turn dazzling white with the
light of the as yet unseen sun. She closed the car doors
gently, the dull thunks sounding loud in the still, cold
air and crunched her way over the gravel to the
kitchen of the house, carrying the mussels. She filled
the deep old enamel sink with water and poured
them in, watching the black shells cascade, listening
to the clatter as they hit the white walls of the sink.
An odd image for the day's end, she thought. But
another day was beginning – she could hear movements in Juliette's room. Quickly she made coffee
and climbed the stairs to her room, not wanting
to be found in a kitchen full of bivalves with no
explanation.

Sitting on the edge of her bed sipping coffee, Axel
knew at last that in bed, swimming through a woman,
she was in an element as sweet, as natural, as water.
As she fell back, already half-asleep, she smiled,
thinking herself – for a moment – stranger than fish.

* excerpted from a novel in progress.

Old Photographs

She had always loved her Grandfather more than she had her parents. Always she had known him more than the others: Mum, Dad, Gran and all the brothers and sisters she had never had. All through the summers of her childhood he had been there, as he had been there after her parents' deaths. Proud and irascible; she would have died for him. Now he was dying in her place. She can do nothing to save him, for he is dying of having lived too long. He had sent for her, above all the others, sent for her to come thousands of miles to this strange coast. The West Coast, where land and lives are cheap. All the long trip from London to Los Angeles she had cried. He had not told her that he was dying, he had just said that someone had to pack his belongings so that he could move to his daughter's house in Kansas. 'I don't want strangers messing with my stuff. I allow only you to come and sift through the rubbish, poke your nose in where it ain't welcome.' But still she had known. She was coming to tidy up the mess of his long years. Coming to say thank you for the years. A week to say so much, a week to say goodbye.

And now, on this last day of this too short, too long week, she is tongue-tied. The rooms upstairs in this racketty old house are empty and sparkling. For days she has thrown whole drawers full of papers, photographs, bills, crinkled greeting cards, into boxes and carried them out to the front of the house, panting and sweating, for the refuse men to collect and throw away. Returning upstairs to wash walls and skirting boards, clean windows, turn mattresses, air rooms, scrape bowls, polish mirrors (ignoring the alien ever-ageing face in front of her), mend fuses, fix catches, take down pictures. She had been ruthless and uncaring, throwing out old jackets, shoes, cracked vases, stained shirts and ties. Unseeing, she tipped out whole cupboards, spreading the piles behind her as she burrowed deep into her Grandfather's past, until she reached the wooden floors of the cupboards and could sweep them out. Then the piles would go into the boxes and out to the garden. The kitchen floor was waxed and gleaming; another colour. She had left only the kettle, two mugs and a couple of plates, saying that on this last night she would go out and buy a take-away to save work. Only the living room remains, in the middle of which, in a dingy, over-stuffed chair, sits the dying man. All week he had grumbled as she swept through the room and out the screen door, heaving the detritus of his fading life in front of his eyes, in ever-diminishing piles. She had left this room until last, not wanting to cause him any more pain, real or imaginary. But now the time has come, the time to tip out the last drawer, the last trunk, empty the last cupboard. She stands behind him, not wanting to start this last pillage, to desecrate his memories in front of him. But there is nowhere else for him to go. His head wags about slightly, drawing her eyes to the cross-hatch of deep, hairy wrinkles straddling his neck. His hair really does seem to have slipped backwards over the years. Now it sprouts in patches down, past his collar, to meet his back, where before it had stopped just below his ears to reveal an expanse of embarrassed pink skin.

'Hey, Gramps,' she calls softly.

The old, old man in front of her grips the arms of the chair with his knobbly, brown-spotted hands, trying to turn around. But still he cannot see her, his body will not bend, where once it had seemed to her to flow.

'Gramps, I'm afraid the time has come, I'm going to have to finish in here. The taxi's coming tomorrow at seven to take you to the airport, I won't have time tomorrow morning.'

'What, you're not finished yet?' He chuckles and settles back into his chair, his hands falling back into his lap. His poor, frail, wrinkled lap. Still, after all these years, she is surprised by the lilting American-accented voice. The English burr has disappeared, and in its place is, what seems to her, the voice of a young man.

'Almost, almost. Just these drawers and that old trunk over there, and that'll be it.'

'Ha, you'll find some things in that trunk. Things even I've forgotten. Can I help?'

'No, no Gramps. You'll break something. You sit there. Do you want another cushion or anything?'

'No. I reckon I'm alright. I'll just sit here and watch you shall I?'

'Do you want coffee?'

'No, I'm fine.' He smiles up at her as she stands over him, wanting to hug him so hard all the bird-bones in him would shatter and splinter.

'I'll soon finish in here, empty things and pack whatever in the case. There's still a bit of room. So, if you see anything you want to take, shout.'

Brushing his whiskery cheeks with her fingers, she turns to the drawers to unpack them, hiding a sudden rush of tears. She is right, it does not take long to tip out the papers and address books and diaries and nams scrawled on pads. The old man waves his hand wearily. Gone, all that has gone. He wants none of it. He does not speak, but his watery, wavering eyes follow her as she throws handful after handful of paper into a cardboard box by her feet. He clears his throat in a body shaking movement and she turns to look at him.

'No, no. Carry on. I was just trying to think of a poem I learned at school. No. It can't have been at school. Maybe someone read it to me? Must've been that: someone readin' it to me. Who could that have been? Too old for it to have been Mum or Dad. I wonder where I heard it?'

She turns back to her task, her body relaxing as she bends over the mess again. She had thought that she had crumpled an address, a piece of paper that he wanted.

'No, I can't remember who it was.' The old man's voice buzzes on behind her. 'In fact I can hardly remember what it was, the poem I mean. Something about coffee spoons. Measuring my life out in coffee spoons. Something like that. "I have measured my life out in coffee spoons." Do you know it? I can't remember how it goes. Maybe I've got it wrong, I don't know. Don't care either. It says what I want it to say.'

Once again the woman blinks back her tears, and finds that she cannot answer him. Steadying herself by leaning on the window sill, she looks out at the bleak landscape. A band of ribbon-road stretches as far as she can see to her left and right. Opposite, there are bleached sloppy shops that slant and lean in all directions. The old paint on the side of the shops trying to attract the passing drivers is so faded that it shies away from the eye. Beyond the shops, down the sandy slope, runs the land, away from those perched on its edge. The Pacific pounds up and down the beach, like some mindless jogger. Pointless. All that sound and movement is pointless, she thinks bitterly. What is the point of it all? What good does it do? As she watches a car screams past, the air howling behind it, turning over one of the cardboard boxes that sits waiting for the refuse men. The papers in the box spill out over the grass and whirl away.

'Gramps, why did you come back here? After Gran died, I mean? Why did you come back to this town? It's awful. It's so noisy, there's no peace here.'

'There weren't any point in staying in England. Only tears there, only memories of your Gran.'

'But you're the one who was English. That's what I don't understand. She was American, not you. You should have stayed at home.'

'What do you mean, "home"?' His voice has

gathered momentum, and he sounds as he did when she was a child, the Cornish accent slipping through, slithering through the years to confront her here, in this shanty house.

'Well, you are English.'

'Crap. Where did I meet your Gran? Here. Where was your mother born? Here. Where was the plant I worked at for nearly thirty years? Here. Don't tell me I ain't home.'

'Well, in that case, why did you go back to England at all?'

'Your Gran wanted to see it. She'd wanted to see it for years. She had all the crazy notions about it, y'know. Tea shops and Dickens. Fog. Y'know. Well, it so happened that your mother met your father at a dance around here somewhere and he wanted to go back to the homeland too. So we all decided to go. Simple as that. Packed up, sold up the old house and left.'

'Gran always said my mother was a copy cat. Do you think she was?'

'What do you mean?' asks the old man, screwing his eyes up against the light from the window, seeing Monica's silhouette against the blank sky.

'You know. Gran married an English man, so Mother just went out and copied her. Married the first decent English man she found.'

'Oh, I don't know about that. Reckon your Gran was just foolin' around. Your dad was alright. He was alright.'

'Yes. I expect he was.'

'Too late to worry about all that child. No use wasting your tears now. Won't bring them back. How about some coffee?'

When Monica had brought the coffee in, the old man was silent for a while, watching her over his cup. She has finished with the cupboards and has opened up the sagging trunk. A leather strap breaks, falls to pieces in her hands, stiff and fragile as cardboard.

'Oh, sorry Gramps.'

'That's O.K. You get on there.'

His eyes follow her as she unloads pile after pile of papers and exercise books.

'What've you got there?' he asks, seeing her poring over a piece of paper.

'Grandad, I didn't know you'd kept all this.'

'All what?'

'All my school books and college essays and everything. Why didn't you tell me?'

'You weren't around to tell.'

But she has not listened to the answer. She smiles, sifting through orange, green and brown notebooks, through blue, black and grey college files.

'Why? I mean, why bother to keep all this? It's nuts. Who'd be interested?'

A sheaf of paper floats out of a bulging grey box file. She picks it up and starts to read. Her body tenses as she throws a glance at her grandfather.

'What've you got there? Come on, show it to me. It's sure making you wonder.'

'Oh, um, it's nothing. Just something I wrote at college. Nothing at all.'

'Come on, hand it over.' The knobbly, turquoise-veined hand reaches out to take the sheet.

'No, no, I don't see the point of you reading it. You won't understand it. It's not an essay or anything. Just something I wrote.'

'I can still look at it.'

He wants to see it, she thinks. I cannot deny him. It means nothing. It will not hurt me now. His shaking hand curls around the edge of the paper as she gives it to him. Holding it at a tilt, at arms length, he reads the piece out loud in his young-sounding quavering voice.

"I will build my language on the skeleton of Sappho. Disinter the bones of her writings: wire the shattered fragments together with the words of a different age. Socket to socket; swivel, turn, bowl away from the charnel house of the bleached bones left by Wittgenstein.

Stripping the flesh from the bones he left nothing but the Idea of idea: the soft-spoken, private language of people who speak when no-one but the other listens, howled away from the grinning cold-dull-skull, swirled once around the hollow-ribbed ribs and away. Then, prising each brown-slush-centred bone from brown-slush-centred bone he sucked them dry. Leaving nothing but a tottering mockery of language – the toothy skull the only reminder of feelings other than a reverence for rules.

I could take a rib from the Scaffolded Man (who is every logical positivist dead-panner; now turning in their graves, smiling to have cheated Death, but horrified to find these fingers tickling their ribs) and mould around it another travesty.

Or I could take a leaf from Sappho's books. The spine may be broken and the pages turning to dust, but still I hear a call: 'Oyah, oyah', croons the mother to her bawling child, 'oyah, oyah.' Unthinking, the mother calls across the semantic desert that is the legacy of those smug dust-bowls. 'Oyah' answers the child, with one spit-glistening tooth pushing through its gum."

The hand holding the piece of paper falls to the arm of the chair. He looks up at Monica to find her staring out of the window once more.

'What's all this mean then? Doesn't make much sense to me.' The old man shakes his head.

'Oh come on, I wrote that years ago. How should I know what was going through my head then.' She follows a scrap of rubbish with her eyes as it flies skittishly through the evening air, gusting with every passing car.

'What's this about bones? I don't understand any of it.'

'Well, I probably only wrote it for fun. Give it here, I'll throw it out.'

'When're you going to settle down? Monica? When you going to settle down with some man somewhere and have some kids? You've been running round for years. When're you going to stop writing foolish things like this?'

'Gramps, that was years ago!'

'How old are you now?' he asks, again trying to pick out her face in the glare of the evening sun, setting behind her. He can see nothing. 'What, twenty four, twenty five?'

'I'm going to be thirty this year. Thirty years old.'

'Well, I guess that makes me older than I thought.' The frail hand holding the paper tries to throw it back, but it flutters to the floor between them. Monica bends and picks it up, crumpling it in her large-boned, strong hand. Then she smoothes it out and, having folded it, puts it in her pocket. She understands more about herself now than she had a few minutes ago, having listened to her own ageing thoughts read to her by the person she loves more than any other.

The evening draws in as she slowly empties the treasure trunk by the window. Her grandfather dozes behind her, his head falling forward, hair slipping over his eyes, long and fine. Monica eases boxes out of the door into the steely-blue night, trying not to shatter the peace of the house, trying to protect her grandfather's sleep. Eventually she has cleared the chest and has only a small pile of photographs left for the sleeping man to check to see if he would like to take any with him. How much can he take with him when he goes?

'You finished? It's getting late.' He has woken behind her, irritable with himself for having slept through these last hours they have together.

'Yes. It's all gone. Here.' She sits by his chair, holding the photographs. 'How many of these do you want, if any? Some of them are badly torn and folded, but I wasn't sure if you'd want them or not. Look through them and I'll make more coffee. Want some?'

'No, not for me. Could you get my glasses? They're in the kitchen.'

When Monica is sitting by the chair once more, the pair of them pore over the cracked pictures.

'Gramps, you never showed me that one!' Monica cries, pointing to a shot of her mother and father on their wedding day.

'Oh, there's more shots that you can't have seen. What about that one?'

An old dog stands sheepishly in the middle of a large field, Monica leaning over it laughing.

'Freida! God, she was old then. How old was I? Eight, seven?'

''Bout seven I think. Must have been, look there's the zoo they knocked down later. There, in the distance.' The hairy, arthritic finger pokes at the trees in the background.

'Gramps do you remember that park? We took Freida there every day, along those red paths. All over. God, I'd forgotten it.'

'Yeah, I remember. It was very hilly, the park was really hilly. And you used to have all those picnics there with your school friends, just next to that cemetery place. You were so funny, you thought the cemetery was the best part of the whole park.' He chuckles as he recalls the pudgy earnest girl that she had been.

'Well, I thought it was. But then it got too big. I remember coming home once from college and seeing it sprawling out further and further. I didn't like it then.'

'Yes.' His head drops back against the chair. He puts his tough palm over her hand which rests on the arm. 'Then you left and never came back. We hardly saw you, Gran and I. You never brought anyone home then; we thought you were ashamed of us. Gran would have liked to see you. Gran was always going on about what a lovely looking girl you were, and where were you with all your boyfriends? I ran out of excuses. You should have been getting yourself a man, she said, not running around with that crazy bunch.'

'They were my friends.' She pulls her hand away. 'And I've hated some of your friends.'

A spasm passes over her face as she realises that she has hurt him. She picks his hand up once more and kisses it.

'There was that one girl you brought once. What was her name? The one you brought to Gran's funeral. Elaine, that was it. I liked her, she was a help to us all.

Like part of the family. But Gran didn't see her, of course. What's happened to her? Do you see her anymore?'

'No, she's in Australia. She's a lawyer.'

'She married?'

'No, no, I don't think so.'

'Now she was good looking.'

'Yes, she was wasn't she.'

Monica stands to stretch her legs, to break the talk, to move away from this name. She goes into the kitchen and pours herself more coffee. She hears the dying man still talking.

'What? What was that Gramps?' she calls through to the other room.

'I said never mind. You won't have to come to show me anything now. No boyfriends, no husband, no nothing.'

'Oh come on Grandad, you'll outlast us all,' she tries to joke as she sits by his chair.

'Shit.'

At last, as she has wanted to all day, Monica cries. Silently, holding his hand to her wet cheek.

'I'm so sorry Grandad. I never thought it would end like this – you and I miles apart.'

'Monica, Monica, why are you so lonely?'

'Oh God!' She bows her head and sobs for minutes without end. Almost choking. At last she stops and wipes her nose with her sleeve. 'I'm not.'

'Oh, come on. You can tell me.'

What do I do now? she thinks. I could tell him everything, holding his hand as I did as a child when I was frightened. Or I stay silent, and let things stay on their feeble keel. He will die unhappy if I tell him. He's right, I'll never see him again. I can't taint all those years. By her feet Monica sees the picture of the park, and next to it a family shot of her mother and her grandparents sitting on a blanket, smiling. Picking it up she sees there is another man there, someone she doesn't know. Trying to divert the old man next to her, she shows him the picture.

'Who's that? That man there, next to Gran? I've

never seen him before.' Her voice flutes up and down the scale as the tear-storm recedes.

'Who?' He peers at the man through dusty glasses. 'Oh, that was a man called Jim. He was your Gran's lover for many years.'

'What? You're joking!'

'Oh, I knew all the time. I don't think she knew that I did, I never told her.' He strokes Monica's hair as she stares at him, dumbfounded. 'I just wanted her to tell me. She never did. She died not telling me. And now it's the thing that I remember most: her not telling me. Strange, how something that wasn't done can overshadow what was. I always loved your Gran, but I wanted her to tell me. To trust me. But now it's like a piece of unfinished business between me and her.'

He stops talking and a palpable silence falls on them. Monica looks away, wrestling with herself as before, wondering whether to explain her loneliness, whether to finish her business with her grandfather. To finish with the truth. It seems almost like a sign. Turning, she sees he has dropped off to sleep again. Having put a blanket around him, she finds herself in an attitude of prayer, wishing that someone would make the decision for her. For hours she watches him, studies him, commits him to memory. The crumpled collar around his scraggy neck, the untidy hair, the broken veins in his face. He, who used to be strong and supple, is faded and enfeebled. Now she looks after him, doing for him what he has done for her. Should she tell him? About her fears? Her fear of loneliness. The night chill sets in as she realises finally that he is slipping away from her. Tomorrow she will be alone as never before. Falling asleep she thinks, dimly, that she should move him to bed. But what is the point? It is warmer here.

Waking to the light of dawn, huddled on the floor, compressed with cold, she finds her grandfather is already awake and watching her.

'Um, I must have fallen asleep.'

'Yes, and I've been busting myself for the bathroom,' he chuckles.

Monica takes the limping, faltering man to the

bathroom and then helps him to wash and change. They do not speak, the coming taxi lies too heavy between them. As he eats the breakfast she prepares, of toast and jam, she finishes the packing, locking the cases and looking into all the rooms for the last time, to make sure nothing has been missed.

'Now, Gramps,' she says, sitting down for a last cup of coffee with him, 'I've put your tickets in the blue bag, the one you'll take on the plane. Everything else you'll need is in there. But it'll be O.K. because one of the stewardesses will look after you to make sure you're where you should be. Then Aunt Elizabeth will meet you at the other end.' Her tears start to come again and she gets up to wash the cups and put them into a box. 'I'll freight the rest of the stuff, or something. I don't know.'

'Don't worry yourself Monica. It's not me I'm worried about.'

'Oh, don't wory about me, for God's sake. I'll be fine. I just wish that I could come with you, but I have to get back. You don't mind, do you? That I can't come?'

'No, it's better like this.'

The door bell rings and Monica jumps, knocking her cigarettes off the table. Walking through to the screen door she trips over a case. It is the taxi. The moment is here, and she can do nothing about it. The cases are loaded into the car in silence. Monica takes a heavy coat into the kitchen, where her grandfather waits, and helps him into it. Desolated, beyond words, she takes the old man through to the car and places him on the back seat. Squatting down, by the open door, she tries to think of something to say. How to say goodbye? How to hold back the tears until he has gone? She cannot say anything. Instead, reaching into the car, she takes his hand and kisses it, as she did the night before. Then she stands and leans into the car, holding him as hard as she can. He pats her back. Finally, she moves away and closes the door, locking her Gramps in. He lowers the window, to touch her, smiling, his pale rheumy eyes watering. The driver gets in and turns the key.

'It didn't matter Monica. I've always known, I've

always loved you, would still have done. You should have said. Then we would have seen you more.'

His hand flaps through the open window, bird-like, as the car pulls away in a cloud of dust and paper.

Stella and Clarissa

As the evening sets in, I find myself staring at a bowl of fruit. When I was a child I used to be vaguely frightened by arrays of dark and glossy vegetables and fruits, and I now feel a twinge of that old fear looking at these strange, bulging nectarines and pears and tomatoes. Skins stretched, nestling curve into curve, they dominate the table. Why are the tomatoes in France so huge, fatly contoured and under-ripe at the same time? The yellow gathering around the scab of the stalk. Turning from the verandah I look over the vast, blue and green valley, sloping with gentle curves away from the house, like a timidly proffered lap. Vines march down the valley sides, and grey and red houses lie half-hidden between gnarled and twisted oaks and beeches. The scene seems to be shrouded in a faint mist, a pall of Gauloise-blue smoke. Leaning against the balustrade I hear nothing but the tacky buzzing of a deux chevaux labouring up a twisting road. Down in the crutch of the valley lies a small hamlet of dusty-grey houses, and, squinting, I can pick out a couple, a very old couple, dressed in dark blues, grey and blacks, slowly walking towards the bar which sits on the only crossroads. Remembering the sprinkling of wrinkles across the bridge of my nose, I stop squinting and turn towards the house.

House? Hut? Hovel? A small, squat, dingy white

square, with dark burgundy paint peeling from the shutters and verandah. One large room behind the verandah, full of the relics of other summers, with one large, lumpy wooden table on which rickety chairs lean for support. A room filled with shafts of light moving slowly through the day, panning the whole room to fade it uniformly. All except a small nook with a pastel-shaded Madonna, piously peering through layers of dust, apologising for the dark creases of dirt gathering in the folds of her pale blue dress. Behind that room, two bedrooms, barely capable of holding beds, and a dingy kitchen lit only by a skylight in which no single pane is whole. At the back, a bathroom; an afterthought. The basin almost blue with the soapy residuum gathering in the cracks of the glaze, and the lever to lower the plug, green with age. The door leads into the kitchen, and on some evenings when lying, almost dozing, in the bath, I have imagined that I was stewing in a glutinous ratatouille, so close is the cooker to the door. A gravel road leads to the side of the house where the car sits, usually dust-covered, but occasionally spattered with the huge weighty splats of rain that herald the electric storms that flash across the valley. Then I must run from the steps of the verandah and skid the car into a shed, rotting in the corners, the original purpose of which can only be guessed. The car, an old Renault 4, smells of all the winters it has seen, tainted with the perfume of pine and cigarettes. The vinyl ceiling is torn and yellowed, the windows scratched and grimed. On the windscreen is a much-scored, lopsided circle in front of the driver, where someone must have cleared the mist of damp mornings with the back of their hand, the diamond of a ring digging deeper and deeper with the years. The seats are covered with a dingy red tartan, grained with sand that itches the back of thighs. The ashtray is missing and one window will not close. In the glove compartment there are papers of the seasons past – Rizla packets, ice cream wrappers, small pieces of crushed foil, scraps of cigarette packets with indecipherable numbers scrawled on them. My second-hand car, bought in

Vauxhall and nestling happily amongst the needles and gravel of this French backwater. Put out to graze by an uncaring mistress. Now I seem to care for it more than I do for many of my friends. A reason to come back every year: to collect my car, and every year realising that it would never return to Vauxhall, but would die on some faceless road.

'Stella! Come here a minute!'

Sighing, I turn from the view. Behind the blue mist the dying sun is throwing a defiant pink flush across the horizon, colouring my skin a child-like rose tint.

'Stella! Quick!'

'Coming, coming.'

I find Clarissa sitting on the bed of her tiny room, her hands splayed in front of her, and her feet jammed into the coverlet by her heels, with the toes spraying out, flower-like. On the end of each digit is a crazy vermilion splash.

'Take your time. Could you pass me those tissues?'

'What are you doing?'

'Painting my nails. And I managed to get some of it on the sheet so pass the tissues and I can wipe it off.'

'Why on earth are you painting your nails?'

'Oh, you'll have to wipe it off – I'll smudge it.'

'Where is it?'

I walk over to her as she sits in a manic freeze-frame of fear, knees up, elbows angled away from her brown body. Immobile apart from her head which wags about, hair swinging, trying to find the drops. As I stand over her I see first her hair and then her thighs, open and straining. The first time for a week.

'Look, there it is. Quick, wipe it off before it hardens.'

'Where? Where? I can't see it.'

'There, right in front of you, by my hip.'

Looking down I see the drops, glistening mica-like on the white sheet. They complete the picture of horror; the bleeding victim on the bed. Actually, more like a procession of ladybirds wending their way across a snowy wasteland.

'What are you waiting for?' she asks peevishly. 'They'll be hard in a minute.'

'They are already.' I scratch them off with a nail, tapping the brown flesh of her hip with each stroke. 'There, they're nearly off. I'll wash the sheet tomorrow.'

She nods, staring at her long fingers, each touched with a drop of blood. Then bends and touches the paint on her toe nails, leaving the faint impression of her fingerprint swirling around her big toe. On the taut tendon of her ankle there is a small white circle where she has scratched a bite and the sun has made no difference. I know that the rest of her body is a smooth, brown country, much-explored by travellers.

'It'll be dry in a minute.' She looks up to catch me staring at her. 'What are you looking at?'

'Your luscious body.'

'Well don't. It's rude. When will tea be ready?'

'Tea? What is this tea? Buns and biscuits? Tea and toast? Angel Whip? Here we have what is known as dinner. And it will be ready when I make it.'

'Please don't talk to me like that. When will that be? I'm starving.'

'In a minute. Why have you painted your nails?'

'I always have them painted. I feel naked without it. Anyway, I've decided to clean myself up a bit. I'm going to have a bath now, and put oil and stuff on. I feel as though I'm peeling all over, and my hair has got loads of sand in it. So I suppose it would be best to wait an hour or so for tea.'

'I was hoping you'd help me a bit. I hate doing all the cooking. I hate cooking. I thought you were supposed to be good at it. And I'm hungry as well.'

'Look baby, if I don't have a bath and get back to feeling a bit normal, I shan't enjoy it anyway. I'll do it tomorrow. I promise.'

'O.K. I'll do it.' I remember the food I bought this morning and almost tell her about the surprise, then turn away and walk out.

'I don't suppose you'd like me to scrub your back?' I ask with faint hope.

'No, thanks. I'll be alright.'

Closing the door I walk back onto the verandah. The sun has disappeared, the mist has thickened. I am angry that I missed the pink-light, as I think of it. It happens so rarely, and lasts only for a few minutes, as though the weather has struggled all day to prepare itself for the moment; then, like a butterfly, it revels in its beauty for fleeting seconds and dies. Behind me I can hear the water gushing from the taps into the copper-stained Leviathan which is the bath. Pulling a chair away from the table, on which the fruit still sits leering at me, I sit looking over the valley once more. Complete silence envelops me as the water gurgles to a throaty stop. No other cars make their way up the beaten gravel track: our house is isolated. I pick up the book I left on the table and try to read it, but the evening is too far advanced. Rather than light the hurricane lamp that swings on the beam crossing the verandah I sit in the ever-growing darkness. Across the valley I watch the probing fingers of cars' headlights bump up and down as they climb the other side and disappear over the ridge, heading for Bordeaux. Saturday night. I pass the offer by. I would rather stay here for hours and watch the disappearing cars roll drunkenly across the landscape. But behind me I hear the lovely Clarissa splashing in her tub.

I can imagine her too clearly. The steaming water flapping around her legs and breasts, her hair strapped to her body by sweat. She would be scrutinising every line of her breathtaking form. Bath time! For me: a long sleep, punctuated with the swishing of flannels and suck of soap. But for Clarissa it is a time of anxiety and hard work. The lotions and unguents, the oils and creams, the astringents and cleansers. And, of course, the nail paint.

What had possessed me that I should have asked her, of all people, to come with me on this trip? This trip, so carefully planned, imagined for months. All that money carefully salted away over the past year, all those calculations of costs, honing down my wants and needs in order that I could lounge on this balcony for, maybe, three months. My little Treasure Island. Days for peace and thought. Alone; I would have to do it alone. I had decided that months before. Then, at that party, when I was so hideously drunk, I had seen

Clarissa through the haze of drink and smoke, staring at me. At the time I had thought she was staring with admiration, now I realise it was disgust. Oh, but she was stunning! The mane of hair, the arrogant thighs. Perhaps it was the thighs alone? Waking the next morning in her austere flat. White walls, sticks of furniture, paintings all seeming to exist on a ... casual plane which I had strived for, yet never attained. Clarissa asleep next to me, her thumb wedged firmly between her teeth. Tumbling out of bed, cursing softly, I made my way through her flat in search of orange juice, marvelling that a flat, that furniture, that curtains could be so disdainful. Wonderful. And in the middle of this stark snobbery lay the big baby on the bed. The picture was so startling that, having wrapped myself in a dazzling white bathrobe, I sat and stared at everything whilst gulping grape juice straight from the carton. My headache nagged at the back of my face, but all I could do was smile. This was it, the flat I had dreamed of, the companion I had dreamed of for years. Finishing the grape juice, I went back to the kitchen and splashed cold water onto my face, looking out over the immaculate, beautifully conceived garden. Astonishing, the whole thing was astonishing. So much understated beauty in one place. Returning to the chair I sat and watched the light change on the walls, listening to the adenoidal moans and snores of the woman on the bed. After a couple of hours she woke with a snort and stared at me. Then, without uttering a word, she disappeared into the bathroom, taking her lovely body with her, closing the door. By this time I had almost convinced myself that I was in love, and, still smiling, I walked to the door of the bathroom and asked if she wanted some coffee.

'No, tea please.'

'Where's the milk?'

'It'll probably be on the doorstep. I didn't bring it in yesterday.'

'O.K. How do you like your tea?'

'What?' Shouted over the sounds of running water.

'I said, "How do you like your tea?"'

'Weak, with milk and three sugars.'

'Three?' The door suddenly swung open, and there she stood clutching a towel around her, water dripping on the floor.

'There's no need to shout. I can hear you perfectly well. Anyway, it'd be better if you don't make my tea, I'll be in here for a while. I'm going to have a bath.'

'Oh, alright.'

I should have known then, when she didn't come out after half an hour. I should have guessed who, or, rather, what I was dealing with: the cleanest ego I've ever met. After an hour and a half the door opened and out she came, looking no different, to find me dressed and ready to go.

'I have to go now,' I said. 'I've got to meet someone for lunch. It's past twelve.'

'Oh, alright then.'

'There's a pot of tea on the table. I've just made it.'

'I expect it will be too strong. Thanks anyway.'

'Right then, I'll be seeing you.'

'Yes. Are you going to Marcia's party on Thursday?'

'Um. No, I hadn't thought of it. Who's Marcia?'

'You know. That short, dark woman in red who was there last night.'

'No. I don't recall a lot of what happened last night. Actually.'

'No. I don't expect you do. You were terribly drunk.'

'Yes.' I looked away, wincing with embarrassment. 'Right. Well, thanks for the coffee.' She stared at me with her blue-blue eyes and walked to a table to write something on a piece of paper. She came back and gave the paper to me.

'Here, this is Marcia's address, in case you want to come.'

Of course, I had gone and Clarissa had been there. I had not drunk as much and woke the next morning to find that the walls of the flat were already bathed with sunlight. The water was running in the bathroom and I left after calling my farewells through the keyhole. By this time I knew better than to wait.

We met quite often after that, and, although we spoke a lot, we never really seemed to say very much. There were so many parties then, it being the beginning of the summer, and there was always somewhere to go. Nothing in the flat had changed, always everything seemed to be in the same place, as though it was hardly looked at. I told her that I was going to France for a few months and she didn't seem surprised. Then, one night at a party in Shepherds Bush, as we were standing in the hallway with people milling around us, she told me she had lost her job, but it was O.K. because she hated it anyway.

'So you don't mind then?'

'No, but I'm a bit concerned about what I shall do now. There aren't very many jobs around.'

'Why don't you come with me? To France?' I stared at her, rabbit-like, stunned by what I had just heard.

'Oh, I don't think I could. I can't afford it.'

'Of course you could. It won't be that expensive, and anyway it wouldn't cost that much more for two than one.' What am I doing? I thought. How can I go away with someone who says they're 'concerned' about their future? With someone who has three sugars in their tea? Whose middle name I don't know? But, the more she argued that she couldn't possibly come, the more I pressed her. After a few days, and many telephone conversations, she agreed to come. I still hadn't seen her that much. I had a rush job offered to me and I had to spend a lot of time on it. But we'd kept in touch on the phone and everything was arranged: she was to pay for her journey and give me some money to cover her expenses, or at least some of them. She didn't drink very much and she convinced me that she wouldn't be bored but would read and sunbathe all summer long. I tried not to think of what I was doing: shattering the peace that I'd worked for, that I'd anticipated for so long. We agreed that if she was bored, or if I felt she should go home, then she would go without demur.

Oh God, that journey down! As I waited at Victoria Station, in the ever-increasing queue for the channel boat I had a sudden, almost paralysing, presentiment about the nature of my partner. I realised that if someone I hardly knew, and seemed not to like, had asked me to come on a protracted holiday with them, I would have immediately declined the offer. I thought of the bathroom in the French house. I looked up in anguish, to see Clarissa staggering along the station with two extremely large suitcases and considerable hand luggage. She kept stopping to hitch up the handle of the bag she had on her shoulder and to rub the inside of her fingers, which were being pinched by the weighty suitcases. She saw me and, with a look that seemed to tickle the back of my neck, beckoned me to join her. The scene that followed was embarrassing and time-consuming. I made her empty the contents of most of her luggage into one suitcase and left it at the checking place at the other end of the station. When we finally boarded the train the atmosphere was strained, not least because I had pulled a tendon or something in my thumb, lugging the suitcase across the station. On the train I had a number of large whiskeys, not attempting to make conversation with the Ice Princess, making much play of holding the glass in my left hand. The boat journey was quiet, apart from the large groups of lads, sloshing their beer around, who came up repeatedly and asked if they could sit with us. In the end we had to move outside onto the wet and windy decks. Then the train to Paris and the trek to Austerlitz. Finally, sitting on the train to Bordeaux, we started talking. In the absence of a party atmosphere we talked about jobs and flats and what it was like to live in London. It was the first time we had done more than gossip.

'Well, if you hated the job that much, I don't see that it matters that you lost it,' I muttered, looking out of the window at the flashing telegraph poles.

'What do you mean? That it doesn't matter? I think it was a reflection on my professional ability. Daddy was furious, I mean, he was the one who got me the job in the first place. He's a friend of the editor, and I've always wanted to work in journalism. I've wanted to ever since I was a child. It was a rotten paper anyway, all the news was so boring. I mean, they must think we're all nuts, wanting to work for them.'

'Why did they give you the push then?'

'They said I wasn't applying myself enough.

"Applying myself", what do they mean? Then I was told to go to Mr Hudson's office. He's Daddy's friend, an awful man. I always hated him, even when I was small. He used to come to dinner with this horrible wife and he'd always manage to get bits of food on his teeth. Then, when he turned around to talk to you, he'd smile and he'd look like a thug. You know – teeth missing. He once told me, when I was about thirteen or fourteen, that I had "nice bristols". I was shocked, I really was. I was a very sensitive young girl, very shy. I just walked out of the room. The next time I saw him was when I started working for him.'

'Go on.'

'Well, when I got into his office he told me to sit down, and he perched on the edge of the desk. God knows how, he's enormous. Then he started giving me all this advice, you know. He started telling me that having a degree was one thing, but getting experience was another. Then he started sort of leering at me and saying that he was sure that I had a lot of experience in some things, but that I'd have to apply myself if I wanted to make it in the world of journalism. Then he went on about all the times I'd been late and hadn't written stuff up. Blah and blah.'

'By and by?'

'Blah and blah.'

'Oh. Go on.'

'Why are you so interested? I don't see why.'

'I just am. Go on. Then what happened?'

'He came and sat on the edge of my chair. Before that I'd been quite polite to him, I mean, I didn't really want to lose the job. But I suddenly remembered the incident about the bristols and I saw red. I shouted at him and walked out. I got my notice that day.'

'What did you shout at him? I mean, did you shout about bristols, or what? Did you remind him?'

'Of course not. I told him that he was slimy and mean and that if he thought he knew about life he ought to look in the mirror some time and see if he thought anyone would let him into theirs.'

'What did he do?'

'He went on about how disappointed my father

would be, but that he could no longer employ me. He asked if I knew how difficult it would be to get a job. I reminded him that I wasn't entirely unqualified, that I had a degree. He just laughed. Well, damn him.'

'Well. It is difficult to get a job, you know. Have you had any luck so far?'

'I haven't looked. You asked me on this jaunt the next day. I'll look when we get back.'

'Yes.'

'Anyway, I thought you said we'd be flying.'

'I would have done if I'd been on my own, but I can't afford to if we're going together.'

'What difference does that make? I said I'd pay for my journey. I don't see what difference it makes.'

'If you'd paid for a flight, you wouldn't have had so much money to give me. We've been through this time and time again.'

'I could have asked Daddy for more.'

'Then why didn't you?'

'Because I want to do this on my own. Mind you, if I'd known it would mean this journey, I would have asked for more money.'

Exasperated, I'd stopped the waiter and ordered some coffee. He kept looking at Clarissa, who just stared back. He poured the coffee and leant towards her over the table and smiled. One of his front teeth was missing and Clarissa burst into laughter. The waiter, misunderstanding, sat down next to her, putting his tray on the table. He started to talk to her in fast, guttural French, of which I could understand very little. Clarissa was still laughing, resting her head against the window of the train. God, I felt tired. The man moved nearer to Clarissa and put his hand over hers. She snatched it away and stopped laughing.

'What's he saying?' she asked.

'What do you think? He's asking you to screw him.'

'He's what? Well stop him.'

'How can I?'

'Tell him to go away.' By this time the waiter was looking at me, puzzled.

'You are English?' he asked, grinning and showing his teeth, or lack of them.

'Yes, we are English.' I smiled as I spoke: there was something too Hudson-like about him.

'Stella, don't sit there being nice to him. Get him off me.'

'Where you go? You go holiday?'

'You go fuck off.'

'Eh? What you said?'

'I said you fuck off. Come on Clarissa. Talk to me. Keep telling me about work or something. Just keep talking and he'll go away. Go on.'

'What do you want me to talk about?'

'Anything.' I moved the tray to the other end of the table. 'Anything at all and sooner or later he'll go away. He's got a job to do and other people want a drink. He can't stay here forever. Tell me about your family.'

The waiter got up and picked his tray up from the table, still smiling. He moved on to the next table and said something to the man sitting there, who laughed and looked across.

'What a horrible man.' Clarissa shuddered and flared her nostrils.

'Yes, he was.'

'You weren't much help.'

'What did you want me to do? Challenge him to a fight?'

'You're supposed to be able to speak French. You could have said something.'

'I did.'

'Yes, and it wasn't very nice. It wasn't even French.'

'It got rid of him.'

'Where are we?'

'Just outside Poitiers. It won't be long now.'

'Good.'

Clarissa fell asleep for about half an hour, to be woken by the stop at Poitiers. She took her thumb out of her mouth and smiled at me. I was surprised. She looked wonderful, like a dirty baby seeing the sea for the first time. I looked terrible. I'd just been to the toilet and seen the grime all over me, and the lamb's-kidney-veined eyes staring back at me.

'Why do you suck your thumb?'

'At the moment there's nothing else to suck.' I looked at her to find her looking at me in a way I'd forgotten. I looked away. The train pulled out of the station.

'Tell me about your parents then,' I said, in an attempt to change the subject as I shifted in my seat. 'Do you see them often?'

Yawning, Clarissa opened her bag and took out a mirror. She just stared at herself for a while, turning her head slightly. Then she started to speak, never once taking her eyes from the mirror. 'They live in Hampshire. Daddy's a businessman. Something in computers. Mummy's a housewife. I left a couple of years ago and came to London. I worked in various shops and did some modelling. Then Daddy got me the job I told you about.'

'Is that all? Haven't you got anything else you want to say about them?'

'No. Not really. I don't see them very much.'

'You've done very well in London to have that flat and everything. It's a beautiful place.'

'Oh, that's not mine. It belongs to a friend of my father's. He's in Belgium, working for a year. I think it's a bit bare.'

'Ah.'

We arrived at Bordeaux and waited for the last connecting train. The vast station was nearly empty as we waited alone on the platform for the small, bus-like train. Clarissa slept with her head on my shoulder, thumb firmly in mouth. When we had caught the train and disembarked at the other end, I looked for the taxi in the village. Clarissa sat on our luggage outside the small building that was the terminal of that line. Finally I managed to find someone with a car who would take us to our home of the next few months. As we turned up the gravel road, Clarissa woke and looked about her. 'Are we here?'

'Yes, this is it.'

'Thank God.' She climbed out of the car and shambled up to the door of the house. 'Let me in. Quick. I'm going to pass out with exhaustion.'

'Um, wait a minute. I have to pay the driver.'

'Quick.'

That was two weeks ago. For the first week we slept together, in the room that is now 'my room'. Then Clarissa was burnt by a day on the beach, so she slept in what has become known as 'her room'. What she was expecting, I do not know. But this little house is not it, and I feel her becoming more and more frustrated. She does nothing and I sit here hating her for it. The light has gone altogether, and I sit in the dark, knowing that she will not leave, at least, not for a while. Behind me I hear the bathroom/kitchen door open as she comes out. The dirty water swirls away through the green plug hole as she pads out onto the verandah.

'Hello. Why are you sitting here in the dark? Light the light.'

'I like sitting here. You can see the whole valley, and all the cars.'

'I had a good bath. I feel more like normal now. I've stopped peeling.'

'Good.'

'Why don't you peel?'

'I've been coming here for years. I suppose that after a while you build up a resistance to the sun.'

Dressed in the same white robe as I wore only a few weeks ago, she sits opposite me. With a towel she dries her hair, bending her head first this way and then that, trapping it between her towelled hands and rubbing it together. The light from the front room spills onto the verandah, across her crossed legs.

'So, you had a good bath?'

'It was alright. There wasn't enough hot water.'

'No. Well, these old houses didn't even have bathrooms when they were first built. The plumbing's inadequate in most of them. They were only built so that the workers would have somewhere to live whilst they built the cathedral we went to see yesterday.'

'I know, you told me.'

'Imagine spending your life shunting yourself and your family around, chasing work. Leaving things behind all the time.'

'It's a lovely church all the same.'

'Do you want a drink?' I ask in desperation.

'No, thank you. And you drink too much.' She is bent double, looking at her calf as she sits on the rotting, cane-spewing chair, and I can hardly hear her. Absent-mindedly she reaches for the glass of wine in front of her. I go into the tumbled, jumbled front room and get out a bottle of brandy. I wonder whether to pour a glass for myself in here, but then carry the bottle, defiantly, out to the verandah. The lovely, radiant Clarissa looks up and tuts. Standing up she sweeps past me.

'It's too cold out here. Let's go inside.'

'Alright, I don't mind.' Seething with impatience I follow her. 'Clarissa, are you sure that you're glad to be here? I mean, sometimes you seem a bit restless.'

'What do you mean?'

'Well you don't seem to do anything. I don't know. You don't read or write or anything.'

'No. I've never read very much.'

'Yes. It's just that sometimes I just don't feel as though we get along very well.'

'Why did you ask me to come if that's how you feel?'

'I didn't say that I didn't want you to be here. All I said was that it's not working out as I had imagined it would.'

'You can put it any way you like, but it makes no difference. I know perfectly well that you'd be happier if I weren't here. Or rather, if someone else were.'

'Oh God, do we have to go through this every night?'

'We don't go through this every night. I'm just saying what I think.'

'Yes, well. Don't worry about it. I was just trying to ask if you would rather be at home.'

'Are you crazy?' Would I rather be at home than here? No, no, I wouldn't.'

'Well, that's O.K. then. Pass us the oil and vinegar and I'll make the dressing.'

'What are we having?' asks beautiful, long-limbed Clarissa.

'Mostly the same as usual — salad, paté, cheese,

bread. Oh, and something I got in the village this morning as a surprise.'

'Is that the smell?'

'Yes, that's the smell.'

'What is it?'

'Moules marinières.'

'Eh?'

Oh dear, what am I going to do with you, my lovely half wit? Only two weeks of this so far, and of those only one week of tenuous amiability. Two and a half months to go. Oh God.

'Mussels. They're mussels.'

'What do you mean, "muscles"?'

'Seafood. Black shells full of soft, orange things.'

'Yuck.'

'You'd better come and see them.'

Lead her through the door into the kitchen, dark and steamy and full of things offering themselves up to us. Racks of bottles, the smell of herbs, cooking and pine.

'Come here, look in the pot. These are the mussels. You cook them in white wine and a lot of onions and herbs and things. They'll be ready in a minute.'

'Ugh, why are they all open like that?'

'The steam opens them up. They're alive when you put them in the pot.'

'They're not!'

'Yes, of course they are.'

'Oh, I can't possibly eat these. They look disgusting.'

'What do you mean "they look disgusting"? They're in their shells, how can they possibly look disgusting? Look, you'll love the taste of them.'

'I won't. I'll hate them. They look all slimy.'

'No, they're not slimy. They're very firm and succulent.'

'Don't, you're making me feel sick.'

'Well ... just try them, at least.'

'Isn't there anything else?'

'No. I bought these as a treat. They're not as cheap as they used to be. Bloody rip-off if you ask me.'

'Can't we go into the village and eat?'

Two weeks yesterday, it's beginning to seem like an eternity. Why is it that it always gets worse when we get back in the evenings? Well, in the day I suppose we don't talk to each other, just peer at things and lie around. Talk? This is talking?

'Clarissa, I can't afford to keep eating out. A meal for two is an expensive business, it's going to use up all my money at this rate.'

'Oh Stella, please. Just for tonight. Please, I can't possibly eat these disgusting things. Besides, I gave you some money. I offered to give you money, when you didn't ask for it. I did give you some. We could use that for tonight's meal.'

'Clarissa, I don't really want to bring this up, but that money will just about cover your journey down here, and your cigarettes for the three months.'

'Well, if you're going to be like that ...'

'Get out a bottle of wine, white wine, and we'll have these. They're ready now.'

We eat in silence. The only noise is the clank of shells hitting the bottom of the metal pan as I plough through the mountain of mussels. They are huge, almost blood red, bursting in my mouth as I bite viciously through them. Clarissa toys with a vast slab of paté, a pained expression on her startling features, drinking glass after glass of sharp, cooled wine.

'Mmmmmm. You should try some of these, they really are lovely,' I say, knowing that I won't be able to eat them all, and resenting the waste and the expense.

'You wouldn't say that if you could see yourself eating. You've got more onions down your front than your throat.'

'Suit yourself. Only I don't see how you're going to discover what you like eating if you don't try new things.'

'You sound like my mother.'

'I feel like your bloody mother.'

'Please don't be rude about my mother, especially when you don't even know her.' Clarissa says this with a shake of her sun-blonded hair that makes the pulse in my groin beat just a little faster.

Pushing my plate away, still piled with the black, ivory-shot shells, I look over the table at my companion, lover, what? She is examining a new bite on her ankle. A small red itching bump on her otherwise very firm and succulent skin. Watching her, I marvel that anyone can be so self-obsessed. Or rather, body-obsessed. It's strange, seeing her sitting opposite me, across the table, sitting where my mother used to year after year when we came here all those summers ago. Nothing has changed in this room since then; the shelves are still littered with the relics of days spent on the beach. When I told my mother I was coming down here for the summer she asked me to clean the place out, to tidy away all these things. Now I'm here, I find that I can't. It all seems so right. I want this haven to stay as it is, as it always has been, for me to come to whenever I want. And what if it all crumbles to dust before I lose the urge to return? Then, that in itself will be right. Reaching for the brandy I notice a dark, russet-coloured stain on the table, near Clarissa. An accident with a knife comes rushing back to me: cutting open a long French loaf, slitting open the soft belly of it, I had cut too deeply and had sliced open the palm of my hand. The knife so sharp I hadn't felt it and didn't realise until the blood dyed the bread a rosy pink. I just stood there watching the red stain seep into the wood, the wood scrubbed so often it was a smooth, almost polished surface. Sucking up my blood. Like a blood-brother ceremony, my palm stinging from the cut, as I forged a life-long bond with this crumbling house. The stain changes colour but it never fades, just flushes angry and dark when I wash the table down, as though warning me that I must not leave. I wonder if Clarissa feels any of this? Feels my attachment to this house? Somehow, I doubt it, for she seems to take no interest in her surroundings, just passively accepts what she finds, where she finds it. It's so strange to see her sedate in her new-found cleanliness, sitting amongst all this grime, in this room that never changes. What does she make of it all?

'I'll have one of those too, if you don't mind,' she says as I pour a drink.

'Yes, of course. Sorry, I didn't think you'd want one.'

Why do I feel so protective of her? As though she

were a small child? She's not so young. In a way it's as though she's a window to the past, through which I can see the different directions I might have taken. I know she will always be young for me, and for others probably. I still don't know why she's come.

'I'm sorry I was a bit snappy earlier. I suppose I was just hungry.'

'That's alright. Could I have a cigarette?' As she lights up, the flare of the match snatches at her eyes, and she blinks and screws up her face.

'Clarissa, don't get angry again, but why *did* you come here?' She stares at me for a while, just smoking and scratching her ankle.

'I wanted to, I suppose. And there was nothing else to do at home, I mean after I lost that job. It seemed like a good thing to do. Anyway, I like seeing other places and all that. I thought it would be fun to do it like this. Every other place I've been I've stayed in hotels, or with friends of Daddy's. That way you never really see anything. I thought it would be a good idea to do something on my own, and not through Daddy.' She gulps down the brandy as if it were water. 'Could I have another?'

'Yes, of course. Help yourself.' She pours a tumblerful and sits back on her chair, legs tucked underneath her, looking out of the window into the darkness. What does she think about? I have no idea.

'And are you glad you've done it? Are you enjoying it? Or would you rather have been in a hotel or somewhere?'

'No, I don't think so. It's strange in some ways. Not having much money and stuff. And not having to do things, or be ready for people. I miss some things, like not having a shower, or going out for drinks and all that. But it's quite nice in a way.'

'What do you think about all the time? When we're on the beach, or sitting here and I'm reading and you're not.'

'I don't think much, I just sit and don't think anything.'

'Oh come on, you must think about something.'

'No, why should I? What should I think about?'

'I don't know. Home, friends, what you're going to be doing in a year's time. Those sort of things.'

'What's the point?' She leans forward and pours herself more brandy. Anyone would think she got through a bottle of spirits a day.

'I'm not saying that there's a point in it, they're just the sort of things that present themselves to you. I mean, you don't sit down and decide to think about something. You just sit down and find that you are.'

'Why, do you always think about things?'

'Most of the time, yes.'

'Strange.' She stands and walks into the kitchen, letting the bathrobe fall open as she passes me. But I know she does this unthinkingly, without design. That I should be so lucky. She comes back to the table holding a large knuckle of bread and smears the remains of the paté over it. Collapsing in the chair again she crams the sandwich into her mouth and chews. This done, she washes it down with brandy. Yick.

'Could you pass me the cigarettes?' I throw them the length of the table. 'Do you want some?' She waves the bottle at me, having refilled her glass. Well, if she passes out, at least I won't have to carry her far.

'Yes, please. I didn't realise that you were so fond of brandy.'

'Neither did I. It's good isn't it?' She turns her flushed face towards me, and smiles. The big baby on the bed has resurfaced. We sit in silence for a while, and I wait, almost with bated breath, for her to speak. I'm sure she's thinking about something.

'Who do you live with in London?' She slurs the word 'live' ever so slightly.

'A bloke called Alex. I thought you knew, I'm sure I told you.'

'Oh yes, I remember now. Why don't you live with a woman?'

'What do you mean?'

'Well, I'd have thought with all the women's lib bit you'd have lived with a woman.'

'That doesn't make any sense at all. Just because I

think that equality's a good idea doesn't mean that I hate men or any of that crap.'

'Don't swear, you know I don't like it.' She lurches forward from her chair and grabs her glass, spilling drops of brandy on the blood stain. 'Oops.' Dipping her fingers in the drops she licks them clean. 'Tell me about him. What's his name?'

'Alex.'

'Yes. Alex. Tell me about him.' Moving the ashtray nearer, Clarissa sits back and looks at me, swaying slightly.

'What do you want to know?'

'Everything.'

'Well, he's a bloke I met in University, when I first went there, about nine, ten years ago. Actually, we met in a really funny way. I was in the bar, about to play pool with a friend of mine. We'd just put the money in the table and I was picking up the cues. For some reason I swung one over my shoulder and I heard this crash and when I turned around Alex was just standing there holding the handles of two pint jars, and at his feet was all this glass and beer. I pissed myself laughing and bought him some more, and we just went on from there. We got on really well. We even did some of the same courses, not that we ever did any work, just spent the three years boozing and playing darts and pool. It was fun though. We shared a flat all through school and so when we left, we thought we might as well carry on, so we got a place in London. I've lived with him ever since, apart from a couple of years when I didn't. I don't know, in some ways I can't imagine ever living with anyone else, or, at least, not being able to live with anyone else as well as I can with him. I mean, we like doing the same things, and going to the same places, so it works really well. Do you know what I mean?'

'What's he look like?'

'It's strange, he's really good-looking, with crazy hair and lime green eyes, and he's always got people chasing after him. You know, phoning him up all the time and all that stuff, and leaving messages. But he doesn't want to know. He's not a philanderer or anything, he's just not interested. All he wants to do is to take photographs. Whenever I see him he seems to have a camera in one hand and a can of beer in the other. He's very good though, at taking photographs. He's had a couple of exhibitions. I can't ever imagine him changing, I hope he doesn't. He's the only person I know who I go out with and just laugh all evening. You know those laughing sessions when you think your neck's going to burst, and your face aches? Well, like that. And when he laughs he sits there with his eyes all screwed up and makes this crazy noise.' I drain my glass and pour another. 'I hope nothing bad ever happens to him. I don't think it will, because I think he's only ever deserved good things.'

'It sounds as though you're extremely fond of him.'
'Extremely fond'? Good God, where does she get these things from?

'Yes, I am. My mother once asked me why I hadn't married him.' I burst out laughing at the memory of my mother's expression.

'Well, why don't you?' I look over, amazed, at Clarissa, who is now slumped even lower in the chair, her long, brown legs propped up on the table, the robe slipping down her thighs.

'Clarissa, I would have thought that even you would know the answer.'

'What? Oh. That. Mmmm. Well, it seems a bit of a silly reason.'

'Jesus, you'll be telling me it's just a phase next.'
'Maybe it is.' She shifts and swills the brandy around in the glass with her forefinger.

'Just a phase? Fuck me ...'
'Stella!'
'Sorry. But I think I'm a bit old for phases, don't you?'

'It's never too late to teach an old dog new tricks.'
'You should know.' Clarissa giggles as I push my chair back and weave out to the kitchen to get some bread. Old dog? That's nice. Leaning against the door frame in the kitchen, more from necessity than choice, I watch her giggling. She can't stop. 'You don't really mean it, do you? About me marrying Alex?'

'What? No, I suppose not. I mean, I haven't even met him.'

'I don't mean that, I mean about other things.'

'Why didn't you ask him to come here with you, if you like him so much? He'd like it, wouldn't he?'

'Of course he would, but that's not the point.' I stagger back to my chair and pour another drink. 'I mean, I know I'd enjoy his company and all that. But three months is a long time.'

'Yesh ... Yes, it is. So what?'

'Well, for a start he wouldn't be able to take that long off work. And I don't think he'd want to. And I see him all the time. And we're just friends ... And three months is a long time.'

'Yes?'

'Well, that's it.'

'You're such a prude.'

'What?'

'You won't say it will you?'

'Say what?'

'Well, I'm not saying it for you.' She tips her chair back and yawns, arms stretched over her head. The robe falls open once more. To cover my confusion I light another cigarette, only to find I have one burning. She's not going to catch me out like that. I stub out the shorter one and stare out of the window into nothingness. Having finished yawning, Clarissa leans forward, elbows on the table, her head cupped in her hands.

'You're very different from my other friends.'

'Good,' I snap. Curiosity overcomes feigned indifference. 'In what way?'

'All this thinking business for a start. The way you dress and talk. Lots of things. I suppose it's just the way you live.' As she mumbles this she traces a pattern in the brandy spilt on the table.

'What do you mean? The way I live?'

'Well, not doing a regular job, taking off whole chunks like this. All the reading and writing you do. You don't seem to rely on anyone.'

'Neither do you.'

'Oh yes I do. I rely on my father too much. I know I'll never actually be destitute.'

'Well, I don't suppose I ever will.'

'Mmmm. Why don't you want a real job? I mean, one that you have to go to all the time.'

'What's the point? If I can do a job at home, in my own time, that seems to me to be a good way of living. Time to myself, free time to myself, freedom to do what I want. All those things.'

'Well, it certainly wouldn't suit me. I like to have something to do each day.'

'Can't say I've noticed.'

'Huh?'

'Can't say I've noticed. You don't do much here each day.'

'Well neither do you.'

'That's not the point.'

'Still, it's nice, isn't it?' She turns her unfocused eyes on me and grins. 'I'm tired. Coming to bed?'

'Yeah, in a minute. I'll just finish this fag.'

She passes her door and walks into my room. I stub out my cigarette and even remember to turn off the lights before I stumble into the room to join her.

How long can I keep up this charade? Not much longer, I don't think. She will see through me. No, no, I flatter myself, I don't think she even sees me most of the time. How can she see through me? I drink too much when I'm with her – that being the only way I can face the fact that she doesn't need me, or doesn't seem to. Why am I lying here in this unfamiliar room, miles from home, watching a still-unfamiliar face sleep oblivious of my fear, fearful because I have only this face to watch for a long time? She seems so different in sleep, not younger, not vulnerable, but at least honest. No frowning, no lip-chewing, no smoke in her eyes, clouding them. And still I wake with my thumb in my mouth. God it's hot, I can hear the sweat creaking between us. Motes flying round the room, flashing in the sunbeams. Why does she want me here? She won't even touch me. If she wants me, why won't she touch me? But she doesn't *want* me, I know that. All that posing last night, just to get her to sleep with me, to get her to touch me, to get her to let me love her. More charades, more games. What will happen today? She'll not allow that anything has happened; go about her business, not noticing my nervousness, not noticing that I'm acting. Why did I choose this mask to wear, unsure as I am that I can continue this? The mask of the disinterested. I'm surprised that she doesn't want me? I should go home, back to London, leave her here in her isolation. If I stay I'm trapped; I peel it all away at my own peril. I can't leave, I can't break the magnet-pull of fascination. I watch her from my mask, my false face of feigned stupidity and make-up, and sometimes see a cracked mirror flashing back. I see in her elements of both myself and my alter-ego. But I know that behind the smile, fumes and words of her presence, is the person who appears in that mirror. We circle each other like wolves, ready to snap. Loping, back-tracking, both lying within the parameter of that circle. Two people wearing the masks they have fashioned over years; fear and fascination the only motives for watching each other. Fear of loneliness, fear of being discovered. When she wakes I will be able to watch the hood fall over her eyes at the moment of her seeing me. Welcome to the vulpine masque.

'Why the hell did we have to do this?'

'Sorry, I just wanted to see Bordeaux.'

'Well, like I said, there's not a lot to see.'

'I just thought, since I'm here, I might as well see it. You can't blame me. I like to see new places.'

'New? What's new about a bleeding motorway? What's so shit hot about ...'

'Stella, there's no need to swear like that.'

'I'll say what I fucking like. It's my car, my sweat that's soaking into the seat and I'm driving through this hell-hole. Jesus! It must be about a hundred degrees outside and about two hundred in here. What a day to do it. I told you they'd all be lemming it, all pouring in and out of the city. Why couldn't you wait till the weekend to see the bloody dump?'

'Have you finished? I mean, can I put some music on now?'

'Do what you like.'

'I would, but I'm not sure I know the way home.'

'Oh come on, you're not putting me through this and not seeing Bordeaux. We might get there before nightfall.'

'Stella, calm down and watch the road. It's only a traffic jam. When we get there I'll buy you a drink and a meal.'

'That's big of you.'

Stella's hands slip on the wheel, slide away; as the car swerves she stamps on the brake; another car whispers past. Stella turns and smiles a wild cheek-hollow smile. (Wolves, wolves.) The women can feel sweat funnelling between their breasts, trickling down their stomachs to soak their shorts. Clarissa's hair sticks to her cheeks and shoulders in crazy strands. She sits as still as possible so that she cannot feel it, imagining her pores opening one after another.

And as they inch forward the little house in which they have spent their time together recedes, becoming more dream-like. The forests around it, the lake which they can see from their bedroom window, fade. The long blank roads, lined with trees and sand, with cracked, pitted edges, become flat, hard, crowded. The smell of pine and salt all but disappears, or perhaps they are just imagining that they can still capture the scent. As they round bends and climb hills they can see Bordeaux before them. Each imagines her life in another city, a life which they had forgotten, but to which they will have to return. The pictures before and behind them flicker, become entwined. The frames judder and freeze, confusing them, making them shake their heads a little, to shake loose the whirl of concrete, sun, shade, metal and endless time. Clarissa, who has little imagination, is not scared. Stella, sweat frosting on her face, is suddenly terrified.

'Let's go home.'

'What?'

'I can't see us getting there before three o'clock. Seriously.'

'Maybe it'll get better. We're nearly there.'
'It won't.'
'Well it seems a bit silly ...'
'I can't drive anymore, not through this.'
'I'll drive if you want.'
'That's not the point. I don't want to go there.'
'I thought you did. Otherwise I'd never have ...'
'You don't understand, it's got nothing to do with this.'
'Well, what is it then? Don't you feel well?'
'What do you mean? "Feel well"? I just want to go home. I've had enough.'
'Do you want me to drive?'
'Yes.'

Stella pulls over and climbs out to lean against the bonnet of the car. A man driving past sees her and whistles, wags his tongue. Stella stares at him, bemused, unsure of what, exactly, he is doing. As she gets in Clarissa jerks the car forward and pushes out through the traffic, bracing herself against Stella's shout which never comes. Looking over she sees Stella is staring ahead, breathing too fast. The journey back is silent, neither of them saying a word. Clarissa pushes the old car too fast, wanting to be back in the safety of the worn living room, wanting to be poised over the green-laced sink with cold water dripping from her face. Wanting to be with the Stella who would have shouted at her driving, who would have run her hand up Clarissa's thigh as she was changing gear, who would have lit two cigarettes and held one out for her. But instead there is this person who is calming, slowly. At last they stop by the verandah and both look sightlessly at the cups that had been left there that morning, slammed down in the haste to leave.

'We're home,' says Clarissa. 'Do you want a drink? Coffee? Beer?'

'No. No thank you. I think I'll just go and lie down for a while.'

Stella stumbles from the car and pushes her way into the house. She falls on her bed, still dressed, and falls further into a dead sleep, livened only by dreams

of steam and tongues and wheels, dreams that she
cannot remember when she wakes up.

'Hello. What's the time?'

'It's late, about eight. Did you have a good sleep?'

'Yes, excellent. Sorry, I didn't mean to sleep at all. I just meant to nap. Or something. Is there any beer anywhere? I'm terribly thirsty.'

'Yes, I went shopping while you were asleep. There's a pack in the fridge.'

'Was it O.K.? Shopping I mean.'

'Yes, fine. Well, I can speak a few words of French. Enough to get by.'

'I didn't know that.'

'I'm just shy about speaking it, that's all.'

'Oh ... Do you want a beer?'

'Yes, if you're getting one.'

As Stella reaches into the fridge she notices that it has been cleaned and packed with vegetables, cuts of meat, fish, different aperitifs. Glancing round the kitchen she finds that everything has been washed and tidied, clothes put away, fruit put in bowls. The table scrubbed. She pads in her bare feet to the window and looks at Clarissa who is stretched out in the last patch of sunsplash on the verandah, her legs resting on the balustrade, black in the evening light. Under her chair a book is splayed open, flat on its face. Stella watches her for some minutes and Clarissa does not move to touch her own skin, does not feel her hair to see if it is dry, in fact, does nothing but sit, watching the cars going over the ridge into Bordeaux.

'Stella, you alright?' Even her voice sounds different as it slips through the door. But Stella cannot let these things intrude; she is dislocated in a way she cannot place.

'Just coming.'

Together they watch the sun dropping, flushing everything as they talk about where they have travelled before, about their school life, about the people they thought they would be. Stella talks sparingly about her family and her childhood, drawing

Clarissa out, exchanging bits of information as their relationship shifts from the known to the unknown. Stella can feel the beer unwinding and then rewinding her, knows that she should stop this, that she should try to re-establish the world that was dislocated earlier, but she wants to know these things. She senses that Clarissa is not what she seems, that there are things to be known which will change other things. But beyond that she feels danger, knows that this is potentially dangerous. Knows herself too well. Then Clarissa throws a net into a silence:

'What was wrong this afternoon?'

'What do you mean?'

'When we were going to Bordeaux and suddenly you didn't want to go any further. You said something like, "It's got nothing to do with this". What did you mean?'

'Do you want a jumper, or would you like to go inside? It's getting cold.'

'You stay here, I'll get them.'

When she returns Stella is looking into the valley, her back turned. Clarissa hands her the jumper and sits down, waiting for Stella to say something, to explain herself. Pushes the other woman with her silence.

'You asked me what happened this afternoon? I'm not sure that I can explain it, it doesn't happen often. But when it does it's almost always the same. It still knocks me sideways, or something.'

'What? What is it?' Clarissa is sitting very still, speaking softly, not wanting to touch and so shatter the scene, to disrupt Stella's thoughts. She could lose her in a moment.

'How can I explain? It's as though everything suddenly crowds around me, all these big thoughts ... Not even that, it's as though all my failures crowd around me. I just feel claustrophobic and want to forget them, want to feel as I did the minute before. I want to forget all the failures. I looked at that city today and saw London and saw all at once the ... sort of ... pattern of my life. Am I making any sense? I don't feel as though I am ... It's just that I can't see any end to it, it will just go on the same way. And do you know something? I keep making the same mistakes. Over and over.' Stella is rocking backwards and forwards slightly on the balls of her feet. Clarissa can feel the rhythm in her own feet, which rest on the same piece of wood. She is watching the other woman rock, cold with the slight fear of what she is hearing. Not wanting to know, not wanting to lose the Stella she has known until now, but wanting to know what it is that makes Stella sound hollow when she is tapped in a certain way.

'Mistakes?'

'Mmm?'

'Mistakes. You said you keep making the same mistakes.'

'Yes ... Today I just felt too hot. Too confused to go any further. Everything kept getting a bit blurred. Sometimes I can't tell the difference between my past and my future very well ... But you know, it's my own fault. It seems I keep trying to make them the same. Do you want a beer?' Stella wags the bottle vaguely and turns to pick up another from the table. 'Do you really want to hear any of this?'

'Yes, very much.' Still their eyes have not met, Stella gliding hers from one edge of the valley to the other.

'I just get a bit hysterical now and then about what the hell I'm going to do. I can't seem to fit in anywhere.'

'What do you mean?'

'I'm not really sure ... The strange thing is that I'm actually supposed to be quite successful, and if I feel like this when I'm successful, what's the point?'

'The point for whom?'

'For me, for me. I just don't see the point of trying to make everything the same; past and future ... And present.' Stella lifts her face slightly and looks at Clarissa, looks straight into her eyes, deep into them. Stopping there, not passing through them.

'Why do you do it then?'

'Why do I make them all the same? Because I don't want to hurt anymore. Because I found out that if you treat things in a certain way, they don't hurt. That goes for people too. On the other hand, I suppose that's why I keep making the same mistakes.' Stella laughs, a surprisingly soft laugh, as her hands work around the bottle and her feet jig. The women sit, not looking at each other, and once again, Clarissa waits. 'Do you remember a while ago, one night when we got drunk, you asked me about who I lived with and I told you all about Alex? Well, I can't remember if I mentioned it then or not, but I haven't always lived with him. I lived with a woman called Kym for a couple of years. It's the only time I haven't lived with Alex. It's funny, the night I told him I was moving out to live with Kym, we had the worst fight we ever had. I mean it was physical. He thought I was crazy to go, and I thought he was just being possessive or something. We wrecked the flat, I mean we smashed it up so badly we had to move anyway. And we lost our deposit.' Stella smiles as she remembers standing in a doorway, tables overturned around her, windows broken, nursing a bloodied hand, as she laughed at Alex spread-eagled on the floor, milk all over him, shaking with laughter too. 'That night we went out for a drink together, because we couldn't think of any other people we'd rather be with. Anyway, I did move in with Kym, to a flat out near Chiswick. It was an alright place ... I'm sorry to go on like this. Would you rather I stopped?'

'No, I want to know.' Clarissa reaches for the cigarettes and settles in her chair, confident now that Stella will say everything, will explain herself.

'We were very happy you know, in that flat. I think it's being here that's brought it all back, you see we came here a couple of times. A long time ago. I loved her very much, more than I should have done. But she was one of my mistakes, one of the things that came to me this afternoon. She's always the worst one that comes. I don't mean that our relationship was a mistake, but what happened to it and why ... I keep thinking of all the good times now, as I'm sitting here. We had a lot. We had a lot of fun.' Stella falls silent.

'What happened? Stella, what happened?'

'Nothing really,' Stella frowns, puzzled. 'There was

one day ... We'd had a wonderful time, it was in the summer. We'd been to the country for a drink at lunchtime and then messed around in Kew Gardens all afternoon. In the evening we went to see 'Julia', the film. We went home and had tuna fish sandwiches and strawberries and cream for a meal. I was watching her as she talked over the table about someone at work and something that had happened there. It was a really funny story and she was laughing, almost choking. But suddenly I caught myself thinking that she wasn't enough, that I wanted more than endless meals at the same bloody table. I kept trying to think properly, trying to remember who she was and that I loved her, but I couldn't. We were together for a long time after that, still having fun, still living together. But something stayed with me from that night — just the thought that if Kym couldn't stop me feeling restless or greedy for other experiences, then I couldn't think of anyone who could ... I realise that all this might sound a bit strange in a way. You see, Kym left me in the end. I often wondered if she knew, somehow, that I thought that. Or more likely she thought it herself.'

'Why did she go in the end? I mean, there must have been something that made up her mind ... Or someone.'

Stella lights a cigarette and sits at the other end of the table, her chin cupped in her hands. The light from the open door to the kitchen gleams faintly over the verandah. The women can see the outline of each other, eyes and hands sparking as they pull on their cigarettes, the white shadow of the paler undersides of arms. The heat has passed and the night, cool now, wraps itself comfortably around Stella, who is feeling the paradox of goose pimpled dark-tanned skin.

'I often wonder about it,' she says, and drinks from a bottle of beer, 'there was no one particular reason. It was all bundled up together. We'd both known other people before, although we'd never been involved in anything so serious. But I had this strange sort of confusion about it. I mean, neither of us were prone to making loud declarations of undying affection, in fact, we were rather brusque about it. It may have been a form of protection in a way, one foot in the door. But, although I felt trapped in some ways, I couldn't bear her talking about her past. When she did it used to hurt me so much, her stories about men especially, for some reason. But I know that one of the most dangerous things you can do to someone is to deny them the right to talk about their past as they want to. So, what do you do?' Stella is rocking still, her arms around her legs, beer bottle tucked between her knees. 'I'll tell you what I did; I ignored it ... Oh, I laughed at her funny stories about it, sympathised with all the bad things and all that. But all the time something was hurting me inside. I did want to know about her past, about what had made her what she was. But I didn't want to know about her lovers, which is contradictory, I know. It was like I wanted to pretend I was her first and last and when she talked about them I knew I wasn't. But I knew that anyway ... it just meant that I couldn't pretend.'

'Doesn't everyone feel a bit like that?'

'I don't know. Do they? Perhaps she did. By the end it got so that I couldn't ask her. We were playing too many games by then. I just can't really see what went wrong.' Stella's voice is breaking slightly staccato through the silence. 'We had a wonderful life, lots of money, lots of friends, good jobs. And it still didn't work out ... Isn't that the right way to do it?'

'I don't know.'

'You keep saying you don't know. Do you think it happens all the time? Things like that?' Stella's eyes are sparkling, with no light playing on them.

'I'm not sure.'

'Why not?'

Clarissa is burning up inside, feeling for the first time what it is to be raw, with no defences, no known means of protecting herself. She is hearing what she had thought she would hear, but that in itself is no protection. What can she say to this woman? 'Why not?' What to say? That hearing about Kym is doing to Clarissa what Kym did to Stella? But that is not the reason for feeling flayed, for feeling the prickings of fear again. How can she explain why not? She feels a deep need to be able to predict reactions, her own as well as Stella's. If not to revert to what has gone before, then at least to something easier than this.

'What's Kym got to do with what happened today? I don't see the connection with having to turn back.'

'Oh, yes. I suppose it's nothing really. I just saw things stretching on in front of me ... I suppose I'm not making sense, I don't think I can explain.'

'Have you seen her since then?'

'What? Kym? Oh, yes. Of course.'

'What was it like?'

'It was alright. It was sad. We didn't really have anything to say to each other. It had all gone. That was odd, thinking of doing all the things I did with someone who had gone.'

'Yes.'

'It all happened a long time ago. I was much younger then. I must have been ...'

'About my age?'

'Yes, I suppose I was.'

They sit in silence, listening to the cicadas sawing away the darkness between their legs.

'Would you have married her if you could have?' asks Clarissa loudly, making Stella jump.

'Yes.'

'Do you think it would have helped?'

'What do you mean "helped"?'

'Do you think it would have helped you stay together? If you'd made some kind of commitment like that?'

'How do I know? I'm not sure, it always seems a false sort of security to me. But I suppose people do it because of children. I don't think about it much. I don't think it does any good.'

'I think it must, it must help in some way, otherwise why would people do it?'

'Straights? I don't know. I always think it's habit. It does seem to be rather habit-forming with some of them.' Stella laughs, reaching for another bottle, beginning to feel rather drunk.

'It does seem to be a logical end to a relationship in a way. Something to be sure of, or something.'

'It sounds as if you think about it a lot.'

'I used to.'

'Why for God's sake? Surely it's something you don't bother with once you know? Like pills and nappies and school fees?'

'I don't know.'

'Why not?'

An echo that is still whispering in Clarissa's mind. 'Because I've never slept with a woman before.'

That night as they lie in bed, not touching, Clarissa can still see Stella's face in the half-light of the verandah, staring at her across the table littered with matches, small green bottles and blue crumpled cigarette packs, as the words settled like dust on the weeks they had spent together. Stella's face: snapping out of its stupor of emotional torpor to gaze at her, stunned. They had both been shocked by what had been said, neither knowing what to do with it, what to do with the unwieldy sentence. Clarissa had coughed and stretched, not knowing what else to do. Stella had left the table, muttering about sleep.

And now they lie here, in the safety of the pitch black, thinking, thinking. Clarissa does not want to lose anything. Does not want to lose Stella, who she saw one night at a party and felt the world shift. She reaches out across the sheets, knowing that if she can touch Stella, if she can rest an arm across her, then she will be able to batten down the static she can feel in the room. But instead of the smooth skin of shoulders, her fingers find tears, as she touches Stella's cheek. They meet in the middle of the bed and Clarissa wraps her long arms around Stella, holding her tight, as if to staunch the flow of tears. Stella's voice is warm and wet against Clarissa's neck:

'Today, what it was on that road ... I thought I might already have had the best day of my life.' And she cries, deep into Clarissa's skin. Cries for a long time, cries for all her mistakes, cries for all the things she'll never know and all the things she won't let herself have.

*

After that night, the two women faced each other in a different way. The masks that Clarissa had seen so clearly had fallen away, and, as they became accustomed to the new people they found each other to be, laughter crept back into the villa, made itself comfortable. The pattern of their days changed, and they spent more time apart. Stella worked on a paper which she was to present when she returned to London. Clarissa walked all over the woods and hills around their land. In the evenings she would read by the light of the hurricane lamp. She started to do the shopping and cooking. She watched Stella work, smiling when their eyes met. They would make love as often as they could, everywhere they could find. Even the pattern of their body movements had changed, now they were lazy and slow and content, where before they had been frenetic in their attempts to satisfy. This lovemaking, Clarissa realised, was the satisfaction of a hunger, a hunger which had started that night. And as Clarissa walked and watched, she wondered about her life as she had not done before, and so she was able to tell Stella on the last evening they were together, as they packed their bags for the journey home, that she was going to move to Sweden to work for her father's firm.

'He offered me the job a while back, but I didn't want to leave London. Now I think I want to do it.'

'You've never mentioned this before.'

'No, well, I wasn't sure about it before.'

'What about the flat?'

'My father's friend will be back by now. I'll have to leave anyway. I think the job will suit me. It'll give me experience. It would actually be a challenge, more so than any other I've had.'

'Oh ... I see.'

'Shall I get the meal now? I know it's early, but we're leaving early tomorrow, aren't we?'

'Yes.'

'I bought mussels, this morning. We're going to have moules marinières.'

Stella follows her into the kitchen and, as Clarissa prepares the mussels, notices little movements, acts of dexterity, which she did not seem to have before. Notices the dimples in her knees, the paleness of the backs of her arms. Small vulnerable areas of skin.

'Clarissa,' Stella's voice is small, 'would you live with me in London? Not go to Sweden?'

'No.' The preparations continue, their rhythm unbroken.

'How can you just say no? Think about it for a while.'

Clarissa turns to look at Stella, and straightens out a cigarette she pulls from her shirt pocket, lighting it from a ring on the cooker.

'I have thought about it, often. All the time we've been here. But I can't. I loved spending time with you here. In fact, I think I love you. But I also think when we get back we should live our own lives. Not see each other.' She flicks her hair, now white-blonde in places, over her shoulder, and removes a fleck of tobacco from the tip of her tongue. 'I can't live with you. You're too weak. I want to remember you here.'

It was at that moment that Stella lost Clarissa, and at that moment that she realised how much she wanted her.

'And Stella, one more thing, when we get home, don't imagine that I made this decision, this decision to not see each other. I didn't. You made it a long time ago, before you even met me.'

Pen the Runt

I have my good days. When I can blind myself to so many things I could be a sleepwalker. Other days? I don't know. It seems so strange. Everything. Out on the streets as I sit in my van watching. Then I know it's a bad day. I can feel something inside – the same as when I was a kid. Like wanting to snap a pencil or a ruler. They had wooden rulers at my primary school, splintered and ink-stained. Snapping them was good. The wood splintered and my hand snapped as well. But now I'm not supposed to snap things. Better to let something inside me snap instead. So, it sits in my belly, crossways, as though it's digging into my soggy sides. Then it winds outwards. Slowly winding, twisted by an unseen hand. Like the babies with flattened noses and crumpled lips, no brain to speak of or with. Twisted by an unseen hand. The babies suffer because they are damaged by a spirit we cannot see ... that's what they told me at primary school. God is not to blame; the suffering children, the suffering of young men (strung out on barbed wire) is our fault. We are sinners.

I never really believed it, I don't think. The teacher would glaze the problem over: 'The problem of suffering, children, is not something we can talk about. We must think of God's life, of His Spirit. And of Jesus, the Son of God, who died that we may live.

He died for our sins.' Then her gimlet eyes would settle on the nearest just-opened mouth, stifling the question. So we were left in silence, still puzzling over this thorny problem. If He had died for our sins ... But no, there must have been an answer in what she had told us and we were too stupid to see something that was in front of our noses! So we were stupid and pinned by Razor-Eyes.

But the glaze has cracked over the years. There is no answer for us to find. And I don't think that we were stupid. People die for many things, in a way neither better or worse than the way he died. Yet still the crumpled babies burgeon. There are no debts to pay, and now I also know that what she said and what she believed are fine. She can say and do what she likes, as long as she doesn't stop where she used to. As long as she shows the little children a picture of Hiroshima and says 'That's man' and then shows them a picture of a mongol and says 'That's God'. Men make each other pay, so why is God so different? I mean, volcanoes, plagues, floods, earthquakes – all that's fine. But babies? He must be sick in the head.

That's a bit what I feel like on a bad day. Feelings come wafting up from that thing spiralling in my guts, like a blast of doubt. I sit in my van hammered by heat and noise and I can see. That's the difference between my good and bad days. But it's not as though I see everything. More like a goldfish with the mind of Hamlet glaring at the bowl of the world. Glimpsing a little the thing made convex. No – it's as though a glazier slipped into my room whilst I was sleeping and took my eyes away, leaving two little eyeholes of thick glass like they put in the front doors of big houses. Someone rings the bell and you peer out to see a large fleshy nose full of pits and dirt. If it's a nose you know then you let it in, but if it's a big dirty unknown nose then the door stays tightly shut and you wait for it to go away. I mean that's all very well with doors – you just walk away and look out of your own eyes. But when you can't walk away, only twist and turn, trying to see all of something at once, those eyes don't tell you anything. Things zoom towards you. And not only noses – chins, ears, toes. Lots of things. I stare disgusted at things other people don't seem to notice.

I see lots of things because I drive all day, delivering clean clothes and towels and other things to people and collecting their dirty stuff. All the bits of cloth they use each week; they wrap it up in sheets and towels and make it into a neat bundle, with four long, floppy ears at the top. Like a baggy turnip. Then when I knock at their door I give them this neat, square plastic-wrapped pillow-shaped parcel, full of white, blue-white, starched sheets and everything. It's nice sometimes, like handing out presents. Some of the people talk to me for a while, very casually, just standing at the door. About little things, like the weather or the size of the parcel or how much it all costs now. Easy talk, and if it's a good day I'll stay as long as I can. But then it's always ruined because they give me the money and this baggy turnip full of shit and dirt. It's difficult to think of giving presents to people if all they give you is money and shit. Sometimes there's no one in the houses and then I leave my parcel in the porch and hope that no one will see it and take it. In a way I prefer that because then I don't have to talk to anyone or collect anything. I mean, sometimes the people who live in those houses are nice and all that and sometimes they're not. Sometimes I think they're quite unpleasant. They sort of look at me like I'm one of their baggy turnips and then they make me feel like one. Then all I want to do is turn and run back to my van and drive off.

When it's sunny there are lots of people walking around and I like driving about, doing all my delivering. Especially if there are kids playing in the gardens or in the road or something. They're funny to watch when they're in their groups, talking or messing around with a ball. You can always tell who's popular and who's not. There's always one kid, and it's not always the biggest, who holds the ball under its arm and points and shouts at all the others. Looking as though they're talking through their nose. I know they'll be the ones who live in the big houses when they're older, like the ones that I take my parcels to. I often wonder whether I'll still be doing this when they grow up and wish that I could tell who they were then, just so I could leave my parcel on their step and not have to talk to them or take their shit. There's always one kid in particular who gets pushed around more than the rest. Some little runt who only looks at the ground or at the ball nestling under the other's arm. I always end up just looking at that one, standing still, not moving in case he or she upsets someone.

It's funny; I just sit there in my van watching them, and sometimes when I'm looking at this runt of the litter I get confused and think maybe it's me. That often happens to me, not knowing if I'm in the van or on the road, and then I get an awful sick feeling, when my legs go sort of weak and I know exactly how that little kid feels. It makes me want to get out of the van and get the ball from the loud-mouth kid and give it to the lonely one. But now I know it doesn't matter how many things you give to lonely people, it doesn't stop them being lonely.

When I was small grown-ups were always taking things out of other children's hands and saying 'Now dear, let Penelope have that for a while, so she can play with it.' We'd stand there until my mother, or whoever it was, had gone and then the other kid would just stare at me. I'd give them whatever it was back. I never really wanted toys anyway. I could never see what you were supposed to do with them. Often I'd just start feeling sick, I mean really sick in my stomach, just watching other girls playing with their dolls. Especially those dolls that had a button on their back and when you pressed it all their hair came oozing out, shiny and dead. Dolls just sit there, with their eyes open and their arms and legs sticking out, as if they're waiting to trip you or catch you out. I know that now children have dolls that move and speak, some of them even wet their pants, and I don't think that's a good idea, because they'll get strange pictures of how real people act. I suppose some of the women in the houses I go to look and act like dolls. I don't think they'd wet their pants if you pressed a button, though some of them look as if they just might.

The other thing that gets me about kids is that they never look at you or anyone. They can be running along a pavement, not looking where they're going, and they just run into things, anything. Dogs, posts, letter-boxes, people. I always laugh when I see that. It reminds me of a time, it must be a long time ago, when I went to an airport with a lot of friends to see another friend off on a long holiday. When she'd gone we all sat down on a long row of plastic seats, just staring at nothing, feeling sad. Suddenly we all noticed this kid, he must have been about five, dressed all in red, apart from his blue shorts, walking backwards, waving to someone. Behind him there was a big, thick, white marble pillar, but none of us said anything or called out. We just watched as he got nearer, flapping this sweaty little hand, and then he hit the pillar, really hard. His head snapped back and cracked a bit. I just howled with laughter. I couldn't stop. Then all my friends started. We just sat in a row shrieking with laughter as his mother rushed up and carried him off. She gave us a funny look and I suppose I can see her point. That's why I always laugh when I see kids fall over, or run into something. I just can't help it.

My mother always called me a tomboy when I was a child, I suppose that's because I wouldn't play with dolls. I would just ride around on this old bike that was much too small for me, around all the parks and commons where we lived. Some of the time I'd be with other kids, always boys, but usually I'd be on my own. I never liked other people being around when I was cycling or thinking, and I always thought best on my bike. Anyway if other people are cycling with you, you can never go whichever way you want to go, you always have to go the shortest or prettiest way. Even now in my van, I go around the long way, or through one of the estate places with broken windows and dustbins everywhere. Part of that is because I think someone's following me and I want to lose them. I mean, I know they're not. I don't know what I'd do if they were. Get out and go into a Post Office probably, no one ever does anything in Post Offices. I just like that feeling. Or going back to the laundry the way I want to go back and not the way someone else thinks I should.

When I get there I have to carry in all the dirty stuff, around to the washing place. I never like that bit, especially in the summer when it's hot, because then it really stinks. I'm always surprised how badly. Those people in their flash houses smell worse than most. All the rich food and perfumes and cigars, and the sweat from their tennis whites. Tennis whites? Don't make me laugh. Most of them are crackling yellow, not where you would see it but in other places.

When I've done that, I walk through the laundry itself, to Mr Kelly's office, so I can clock off. It's nice walking through there, with all the machines going, spreading and folding all the white cotton, and it's always noisy with the machines and people shouting. I like it because then I feel like I'm a part of it, like being a part of a much bigger machine. There's a woman there called Mrs Kaffee who always smiles when she sees me and shouts, 'Hi Pen! Good day?' I just smile and nod, even when it's been a bad day, because I think she's got a terrible job, heaving wet sheets onto the spreader and I don't think she wants to know about my bad day. She's been there for twenty-three years, which is difficult for me to imagine, since I must have been about four when she started there. When I think of all the things that must have happened to me and when I try to think of her just standing there heaving wet sheets around the whole time, it makes me feel dizzy. When I've smiled at her I go into Mr Kelly's office to sign the book and give him the day's takings. He's a funny man, he wears a green visor and those metal arm bracelet things that keep his shirt sleeves rucked up around his shoulders. I always want to give him a cigar when I see him sitting there like that but he's much too serious. He counts the money, never saying anything, and passes me the book to sign and then I walk out. I always say goodnight and sometimes he answers, but usually he doesn't. I've never worked out what he does in there, or why he's so important. It's Mrs Kaffee and all her friends that do all the work, all he does is count the money.

I walk back to my rooms, they're quite near the laundry. In fact, I can hear the machinery in the mornings when I wake up and whilst I'm getting dressed. I have to climb five flights of stairs to get to my rooms and when I get in I just fall on my settee and pant. That's because I always make sure I run up all the stairs' ninety steps, since I think if I can do that and not die, then I'll live for at least one more day. I put my coat away once I've stopped panting and put the kettle on for tea. If it's really hot I'll have a can of beer, but I try not to do this very often since I used to drink a lot, and now I've cut down. Quite often I'd find I couldn't walk down the stairs in the morning, after I'd been drinking the night before, let alone run up them. That worried me because then it was as though I had no guarantee of living much longer. So I cut down and now I have a couple of cups of tea.

After I've read the paper, which I buy on the way home, I have a cigarette and just sit in this tiny kitchen bar I have at the end of my sitting room, thinking about things. Reading the paper depresses me a lot, there's too much cruelty and arrogance in the heads of the men who decide things. Like where to put missiles and how many to put there, and in their photographs they look as though they're smirking about something. As though they've made a white queen sit on a black king's face, the world a great big chess game. Which is something that makes me feel inadequate, sitting there smoking my cigarette. I can't even play noughts and crosses. It cracks me up sometimes, you can look through a whole paper and not even see a picture of a woman, or if you do, it's because she was found murdered on some road somewhere the night before.

That time of evening is odd. I feel sort of exhilarated by the thought of all the hours I have in front of me before I have to walk to the laundry, and yet there are always too many to fill. I often think it's a shame that I don't eat fancy food. In fact I don't eat much at all. If I ate lots of frilly things then I'd have to spend hours preparing them which would kill the early evening, that bit being the worst. But if you live on your own it's not really worth it, so I just eat cheese and salad or open a can of something. I know I should make more of an effort, but there isn't any point. Even when I go to restaurants I just eat steak or chicken or something plain. I know that's partly because I'm not sure how to eat things like asparagus or mussels or other things in front of other people. I remember seeing a man eat an artichoke in a flash place years ago and I just thought it looked obscene. So, by the time I've eaten and cleared away it's still early.

Most evenings I read, lying on my settee, listening to the radio. I have lots of books, and I get at least three out of the library every week. I read women's books mainly. Margaret Atwood, Alice Walker, Marge Piercy, Rita Mae Brown and other writers like them. They're good books and they make me feel better because then I know that other women feel like I do. After a couple of hours my concentration wanders, however good the book is. I start to think about the day I've had and the day to come. Even though they're all pretty much the same, there's always something different about them. It can be something really small, like buying a book, or Mrs Kaffee forgetting to say hello.

But usually I think about the women I have seen. You see, when I see some women, I get a thumping feeling and want to walk over to them and get to know them. But it's not just that. I want to touch them and be able to watch them. They needn't be pretty or anything. It can be a woman pushing a pram, with a couple of brats holding on to her coat and pulling and shouting. And maybe she's young and looks as though she hasn't slept for weeks. Then I want to get out of my van and prise the children away and push the pram back to her house for her and talk as we walk along. Women, girls, like that make me feel terribly sad. They make me want to wrap them up in soft stuff and plump them up, fill in all the hollows they have all over them. Of course it's not only feelings like that I have. There are women at bus stops, or standing in a phone box or walking out of a building, who look at me and through me. Maybe it's the way they walk or the way they're holding a bag or the way they touch their hair, but they make me think of something completely different. They make me think of sex. I just want to walk up to them and stare at them and wait for something to happen.

Those are the kinds of things I start to think about as I lie on my settee, reading. After a while I can't stay still any longer and I wander about, in my three rooms. My bedroom, living room and bathroom. It's all very bare and a bit dirty. All I've got are books and a few clothes. I'd like to fill it with things, but if I go out to look for furniture or pictures or anything, it never seems worth it. I'd have to buy a lot of stuff before it made any difference, and the thought depresses me. I bought a yucca tree a while ago, even though it was so expensive. It's in the middle of the living room and I walk around it a lot. I look after it well because I'd hate it if it died. I know I'd never buy anything again. But walking around those rooms isn't enough after a while. Then I run down the stairs and go for a walk, even in winter. There's a common down the road, which is dark at night, but I don't care. I walk for hours, along these paths, passing ponds and tennis courts and people's back gardens. I try to think of which route I'd take if I were a kid again on my old bike. But now I've covered all the routes, so that's not much fun anymore. I know the common so well I could walk around it with my eyes shut. I've been walking round it every night, almost, for a couple of years.

I know that walking like that only stops me thinking for a while, soon my mind starts up where it left off. I've tried not to go for these walks, forced myself to stay in all night. But then, when I go to bed, everything starts churning, my mind, my stomach, everything. I just lie there shaking, my head sort of spinning. It's like I'm about to do an exam, or about to go on stage. I keep yawning, but it's not sleepy yawning, it's nervous yawning. Even if I try to make myself realise that there's nothing to be frightened about, it doesn't help. I do this thing where I lie straight in the bed, like a board, and relax from my toes upwards. I think about every bit of me, not just my feet and arms and all the bits I can see, but about my liver and spleen and kidneys and veins. Everything. I make them relax by talking to them, and if they listen it's like a sherbert fountain whizzes through them and then they lie still. I always leave my face till last, because it's the most difficult bit. My neck's always rigid and like wire, so I start with that and then think about my eyes and nose and chin. But by the time I get to my mouth and teeth, the rest of me's all tight again, so it's all pointless. I start imagining that I'm suffocating or dying of malaria or AIDS or something and then I have to get up.

Once I'm up and all the lights are on I'm O.K. again. I know I'll live for another day, which is a sign that I'm getting better. It used to be that knowing that would only make me feel worse, because I didn't see the point in another day. You know that song by the Beatles, 'Another Day'? Well, I don't like the Beatles at all, but that song is wonderful. I used to listen to that all the time, until I wore the record out. I decided not to buy another copy because I knew it so well it was as though I had it in my pulse somehow. I suppose it's a bit like the books I read; it's good knowing someone else feels the same way. I know it's just a song and that the men who sang it were very rich and secure and all that, but I don't think that makes any difference. Maybe a lonely woman told them how she felt one day and they went away and wrote about it. If that's what happened, then she must feel a lot better about things.

My doctor in the hospital had a name for my not-being-able-to-sleep feeling. He called it an anxiety attack. He said it happens when I try not to think of things and keep them all inside me instead, like a rubbish tip. He said that they come back later, very distorted and confused and stop me thinking normally, then I get worried about things that another bit of me knows will never happen. The rational bit of me, in my mind. He said that I ought to sit down and try to think calmly about whatever is bothering me. I tried to tell him that some of the stuff I had in me was so nasty and upside-down that I never wanted to think about it. But he made me talk about it all the same. I think he thought like a lot of people do; that if you talk about things and discuss them then they sort of dwindle to nothing. I've never been sure about that. I mean, he made me remember bits of my childhood and schooldays that I'd buried completely. Surely the reason I'd buried them was because I didn't want to even think about them, let alone talk to someone I hardly knew about them? But if you don't tell them anything then they never let you go. They just keep giving you pills and take your clothes away, so that you don't even feel like a person anymore.

It made me feel very vulnerable sitting in a really small cotton dressing gown thing that didn't even cover my legs. And I've always had this thing about my legs. I used to play lots of sports, so they're all packed with muscles and scars, and one of the ankles is always a bit puffy from one time when I really damaged it. So they don't even match, I mean they're not like a pair of legs because they don't even look alike. And so I'd be sitting there, feeling miserable and smaller and smaller, trying to cross my legs and stop my tits from falling out of this skimpy gown, which wasn't even mine. All I tried to do was to think about what they wanted to hear, try to think of things to say which would make them give my clothes back. And always in the back of my mind would be this picture of a couple of white doors with bolts and a blood red sign on them, because I knew that in there was the machine that they used to shoot all that electricity through people. It used to worry me most because when people draw electricity they always use small, pointed arrows and the thought of millions of arrows ripping through me would make me feel weak.

Also, I'd seen that film where Jack Nicholson goes to a hospital like the one I was in, and all through it he stays himself. I mean he doesn't spend all the time trying to think of what they want to hear, he just goes on doing all the things he would have done anyway. Like when he takes them all fishing, and they all seemed so happy and almost normal. And there's that bit in it when the big Indian guy suddenly says something. He's been pretending to be deaf and dumb, and suddenly he says something. He'd beaten them all in there by pretending to be something he wasn't all the time. You see, you really can't tell what to do when you're in a place like that. Anyway, in the end Jack Nicholson gets a bit of his brain cut out, a lobotomy or something. He's as good as dead, especially with his crazy eyes shut. When I remembered that film I'd get worried. But all I could think sometimes was that Jack Nicholson wouldn't have been able to take them all fishing if all he'd been wearing was a tiny dressing gown. Maybe all the doctors in my hospital had seen the film too, and that's when they decided to take everyone's clothes away.

I used to have to see my doctor four times a week, to sit in his room and talk for a couple of hours or so. I could never think of anything to say at first, which would embarrass me, because it was like a social occasion or something, with me being tongue-tied as usual. After a while I stopped giving a damn, when I realised that I really wasn't a person for him, just an interesting case. Don't think I'm trying to make out that my case was more interesting than other people's. It's just that we were all cases and not people. He'd always start the discussion off with some question about my family. In fact that's about all he wanted to talk about the whole time I was in there. For the first month or so all I'd do was describe them, what they looked like. My mother, father and brother. It was funny, I'd lived with them for nineteen years and I'd never really thought about what they looked like.

I realised that my mother has a face that's sort of pushed in, like someone pushed her nose right in when she was a baby. And she had all this make-up all over her dresser back at home, which she'd experiment with all the time, trying to make her nose look like everyone else's. I always thought that was bloody silly. By the time she'd finished it was always light and dark in patches, and then everyone would stare at it and realise that it was all caved in. She was always asking me if I wanted to experiment with her make-up, but I never wanted to. I didn't see the point of putting cream and powder all over my face, and she'd get upset about that. She'd try to make out that I was less of a girl or a person or something because I wasn't interested in clothes or make-up or any of the things she liked. She'd sigh and tell me I'd regret it when I was older and all my friends were going out with their boyfriends. Regret what? What was it that I'd regret? I'd ask her. But all she'd do was sigh again and smile sadly at me. I did try a couple of times to please her, but I just ended up getting angry with myself and then with her. It's not that I don't like her, I love her, it's just that we don't get on very well. I'd never do anything she wanted and it was like she was always giving me things she'd taken away from other people, which I'd just give back when she'd gone.

My father was different, and still is I suppose. I say was because I don't think of them, my parents, being is anymore. I stopped thinking of them being is when they took me to the hospital and left me there. But anyway, my father was much older than my mother and very tall and distinguished looking. He was born in Germany and moved to London with his parents when he was small. I always thought it was funny him really being German because he was the most English person I've ever met. He'd only ever eat Cooper's marmalade, drink Gordon's gin, smoke Benson and Hedges cigarettes and wear tweed jackets and all that stuff. Later he took to smoking a pipe which just about completed the picture. I mean, he looked like Sir Conan Doyle must have done, or someone like that. I never saw him very much, because he was always working, and I never worked out what he did. I know it was something to do with banking, but that doesn't mean much. The way I look at it, everything's something to do with banking. When I was about fifteen he got arthritis in his left leg, and had to walk with a walking stick. It was sad really, because he'd always been into fitness and posture and all that. It was sad to see him standing there looking like he had a rod for a backbone and knowing that he had to rely on a piece of wood to do it. I don't think he liked me much anyway. All he used to say to me were things like, 'Shoulders back', 'You shouldn't be eating that muck' or 'What are you doing inside on a beautiful day like this?'. You see what I mean, it was never anything positive, always some kind of criticism. I think I stopped noticing him after a while. His voice got like some kind of background buzzing that's easy to ignore. I think Gordon and I got our height from him, because mother is small as well as being dumpy.

Gordon is my brother. It hurts to think of him. When I talked to my doctor about my family it was easy to talk about my parents. In a way they'd stopped being important when they stopped being is. But when I started to talk about Gordon I'd always cry. You know when tears just sort of fall out of your eyes, without making any difference to your voice or your throat? When they just trickle out and tickle your cheeks? That's how I'd cry then. Just sitting there, talking about him. Like I had a great lake inside me that was slowly dribbling out, endlessly. Clutching at my dressing gown that would get wetter and wetter where the tears fell off my face. And the doctor would just keep on and on at me to talk about him. It's very difficult to talk about someone who you used to love more than anyone and who you just can't bear to think about now, they've changed so much.

He was one of the prettiest children I've ever seen, and was always sweet. He had blond hair and blue eyes, just like me. Everyone was always saying what beautiful children we were, and I suppose we were. I mean we were nice too. We never fought or anything, and always shared things. He was only a couple of years younger than me, and so I could talk to him like I'd talk to anyone. I never minded if he came cycling with me, in fact I used to like it so much, I'd ask him to come. It was great when we cycled next to each other, pushing pedals in motion at the same speed. I'd look over at him and catch him smiling, especially if we were free-wheeling down a hill with our legs sticking out in front of us. We'd always start shouting at the same time, sort of yodelling or something, as we got faster and faster. So I enjoyed it a lot if he came with me. We even went to the same primary school for a while when we were small, dressed in the same uniform. It was a small mixed school, with lots of fields around it. My father's chauffeur would drop us off at school and we'd walk in with the other children but we always felt different. As though there was a long piece of elastic between us that could stretch for miles and keep us in touch however far apart we were. All the other children seemed very alone to us.

At lunchtime when we were allowed to play in the fields, we'd just sit on a step somewhere, next to each other, sometimes talking, sometimes not. The other children would leave us alone. I think they were scared of us because our father was so rich. Which always seemed very silly to us, but if they thought that it made a difference then they must be silly anyway, so we wouldn't want to be friends with them. Sometimes I think I was happier then than I have been ever since. Just sitting on a step with Gordon in the summer, watching other children playing.

After a couple of years, though, Gordon was sent to prep school, the same one that my father went to, and he had to board there, so we didn't see each other so much. At first it was horrible, I hated having to go to school on my own, because I hadn't bothered to make friends with anyone else. And when he came back during the holidays, it was always difficult for a few days. I mean to think of anything to say. But after a while it was alright again, like he'd never been away, and we'd go cycling and swimming and things. Soon after he went to prep school I left the primary school with the steps and the fields and went to a girls' grammar school further away, but I didn't have to board. I think it was then that Gordon and I started to grow apart.

We still looked pretty much the same, but he was getting a harder face and I seemed to get taller all the time. He stopped talking to me for a while when I first went, I don't know why. I didn't mind that school. It was much bigger than I expected and there were a lot more girls than I thought there would be and they seemed very grown up and mature. I liked all the lessons though and won lots of prizes at the end of the year, for sports as well as exam results. By the time I was in my third year Gordon was in some public school miles from London and I would hardly see him at all.

It was then that all this trouble started, or that's what my doctor said. I told him all about my primary school and when Gordon and I got along well without much trouble. I mean, up until then I think I just did things that everyone did. He must have heard stuff like that loads of times, everyone is like that. My trouble stems (my doctor's word) from my friendship with Elizabeth, who I met in my fourth year. She was beautiful and funny and athletic and intelligent, all the things I wanted to be. At first I didn't really notice her, but after a while I did and whenever she walked in I'd get this thumping feeling in my stomach and would want to get as near her as possible. I even managed to tell my doctor about how much I liked her without much trouble, no crying or long silences while he just sat there, or anything like that. It was all the things that happened after we got friendly that took ages for me to tell him. My doctor wasn't allowed to prompt me or anything, he just sat there and waited until I realised that I'd have to tell him or I'd never get out of there.

You see, Elizabeth and I got to be very good friends. We'd sit together in lessons and walk down to the bus stop together and go to tea with each other all the time. But I knew somehow that the way I felt about her was different from the way she felt about me. I'd find myself watching her all the time, especially in games lessons, and getting my stomach-thumping thing when she moved in certain ways. I'd go home and worry about it a lot but I never told anyone. I would have told Gordon, but he was getting more distant all the time, although we still got on alright.

One day something happened which I still remember like yesterday, although it must have been ten or twelve years ago. Elizabeth and I had stayed on after school to practise our lacrosse one winter's evening.

Afterwards I asked her to come back to my house, which was nearer than hers, and have tea and then the chauffeur could take her home, rather than her going home in the cold. When we'd walked back to my house, we were freezing. I mean we'd been out on the pitches anyway and it was very cold. So I made some hot chocolate and got out some Kunzel cakes for us. It's funny how I remember that they were Kunzel cakes, but as I said I can remember a lot about that night. We took the drink and cakes up to my room and, for some reason, I suggested that we sit up in my bed and eat them, to try to get warm. I knew I'd like to sit in bed with Elizabeth, but I also knew that I'd never touch her, she was far too beautiful to touch. It was whilst we were in bed that my father came in.

It's strange, I couldn't tell my doctor about this for months. Even if I tried to explain, I just couldn't get the words out, I'd just sit there stammering. I wasn't crying or anything, I just couldn't actually say the words. It's very frightening if that happens, when you want to say something and can't. My arm would always hurt too. That's because when my father walked in he didn't even say anything, he just pulled Elizabeth out of the bed and shoved her through the door, shouting down the stairs for the chauffeur to take her home. Then he came back into my room and almost ran over to me, pulled me out of bed by my arm and started to hit me. He had his walking stick by then and that's what he used to hit me with all over. I kept trying to move away, but he just held on to my arm. All the time he was sort of quietly shouting words that I couldn't hear. I know one of them was 'pervert' and he kept saying, 'filthy, filthy'. It hurt so much in the end I passed out, but a bit of me realised that he just kept on hitting me. When I finally woke up I was on the floor of my room, and it was dark. I could hear my parents shouting downstairs, but not what they were saying. I couldn't move, but I didn't really want to anyway. One of the strange things about that evening was that I didn't cry at all. It seemed like too much of a small thing to do. My arm was twisted beneath me and I couldn't move it, but I thought that was just because I didn't want to move at all.

I only ever start crying when I think of the next bit. I heard Gordon coming up the stairs and walking towards my room. I thought, it seems funny now, but I really thought he was coming to see me. Instead he went into his own room and started to play some music. I passed out again listening to it and wondering if he knew where I was. It wasn't until the next day, when mother came to see me in the morning that we found out my arm had been broken. That's why I can't bend it properly now, because I lay on it all night. When my mother came in that morning she was all red around the eyes and her face looked more pushed-in than usual. She hardly said anything, except to the hospital on the phone. Then she just held me all the time we were going there, which hurt my arm but it was nice of her.

I never saw Elizabeth again. I didn't go back to the same school after my arm had mended, I was sent away to a boarding place, like Gordon. I know now that was because my father couldn't bear to see me anymore. All he cared about was Gordon. But that didn't matter because I don't think I cared anymore. At my new school I met Jane and by then I knew exactly what I wanted and what I was called. It's funny. I know that I loved Jane a lot, but when I think about her now I just smile because everything I did to her I did thinking of my father and how much it would hurt him. My doctor told me that this feeling was one of the feelings I had to get rid of. The feeling of doing something to spite my father. Sometimes I wonder whose side that doctor was on, although he would say that it wasn't about taking sides.

One of the best times I had in that place was one afternoon when I was talking to the doctor about that, and we'd been discussing it for months, and he told me to forgive my father. He had almost convinced me that I should, I mean I was teetering as I sat on the chair holding my dressing gown. Then I suddenly said, 'No, I won't. Because I don't give a shit about him.' I think saying that kept me there longer than I would have been otherwise, but it was worth it. The doctor had never heard me swear before, because I don't usually. We were never allowed to at school or at home, so I never got into the habit. He just looked really shocked and never mentioned it again.

Other patients in the hospital were always swearing. Just going on and on in swear words. I always found it very boring becaue there aren't that many that you can string together. I know a lot of them thought I was a snob. It's strange, it doesn't matter where you are, there are always class divisions. Even in a ward of a mental hospital there are class divisions. You really can't get away from them. The only time I ever managed to get away from them was when I spent a long time in Europe. I went there after I'd finished my boarding school. I almost didn't bother to go home before I left for France, but I needed some money. That was one of the last times I saw Gordon. I was really shocked. He came into the kitchen one morning, the day before I left for France, and he looked completely different. His eyes were hard and his hair was very short. He'd got as tall as my father and was very thin and erect and well-dressed. He just looked at me and nodded, then he wished me a good holiday and walked out. I didn't think much of it, I didn't have time. Now I often wish I'd run after him and talked to him. I didn't know I'd only see him one more time. I left the next morning.

I think the time I had in Europe was, perhaps, happier than the time I had in primary school with Gordon. I always wanted to talk to the doctor about it, about Florence and Paris and Vienna and Athens. But he didn't want to know about when I was happy, only about when things weren't going well. Everywhere I went I was happy I suppose. All the different foods, landscapes and architecture. Just so much that was different. And all the women I met. I'd never known that there were so many women like me, or that you could be happy about it. I'd read *La Bâtarde* when I was at school and imagined that everyone felt like that. But they don't. My arm hurt a lot then, which was the only bad thing about it. It would hurt whenever I was in bed with a woman. After a while I started to worry about it and I went to see a doctor when I was in Spain. But that didn't do any good. He didn't look at my arm, he only wanted to examine my breasts.

Then someone explained to me about people in the war who'd lose their limbs and later imagine that they had pains in them, when they weren't even there. I know my arm was there and all that, but it still felt strange. I started to dream about my father coming into the room where I was and beating me again. Quite often I'd wake up to find my lover holding my arm to stop me beating it against the wall. It was towards the end of that year that I started having my anxiety attacks. When I couldn't sleep but would lie awake, or half-asleep, trying not to think of anything. But always I'd end up imagining my father hitting me with Gordon watching at the door. My doctor told me that my thinking that meant I really wanted to sleep with Gordon. But I don't think that's true, all I ever wanted was to keep on loving Gordon. I just found that I couldn't.

I had to come back to England because I was going to university to read philosophy. I really like philosophy. The idea of all those loops in time and space. I used to imagine crawling through them and coming out into a world where my arm didn't hurt and Gordon was still ten years old. I went back home to collect all my stuff and get myself ready. My mother was the only one who talked to me and all she would say was how thin I was. I was very thin. I suppose I hadn't noticed it, I don't think you ever notice anything about your own body except how much you dislike it. I took a friend of mine called Lydia home with me, a woman I met on the train back from Athens. I told her she could stay overnight in our house, because she had to go all the way up north to Manchester to get home. That's another thing I regret, like not running after Gordon that day a year before.

Because that night is another night I can't forget. Not because it was violent or full of pain or anything. It might have been better if it had been. Whenever I think of it the tears fall down my face like they did at the hospital. I don't think it will ever get any better. I mean, however much I think about it or discuss it, I'll never be able to erase the memory of Gordon's face and the look on it. He came into the study when Lydia and I were sitting in there. I'd told her about my younger brother and how lovely he was, but that was mainly to convince myself. He stood in front of the two of us and just looked. I know we were sort of dirty and scruffy, we'd just spent five days travelling, but I couldn't believe the look of disgust on his face. I just stared back at him trying to remember where I'd seen him before. I mean, he didn't look like Gordon. Then I realised where I recognised him from: every Second World War film I'd ever seen. He was wearing a black shirt with epaulettes and a black tie, with black jackboots over his trousers. And on his shoulders were these silver swastikas. He looked gorgeous, with his blond hair and blue eyes, watching me with my blonde hair and blue eyes. He started to speak, not to Lydia, he just ignored her. He sounded like my father, but angrier. He just told me that if the world was made as it should be, then I'd be gassed along with all the other perverts and that if he had anything to do with it I would be when the time came. There was more, much more. But I didn't listen. I just started shaking and my arm felt like it was on fire and I kept seeing Gordon watching my father and I. I must have started screaming because Lydia was hitting me to stop and Gordon had gone. My doctor told me I've exaggerated Gordon and his appearance. But I haven't. It was like that. How would he know? He wasn't there. Gordon left school and went to work for the National Front. I think my father was proud of him.

After that evening nothing was ever the same again. I never felt anything except my arm. I never felt anything for people. Oh, I went to university for a while and all that. But it didn't work. I forgot to eat or sleep. I never talked to anyone and if any girls came near me or tried to talk to me I couldn't answer. I'd just walk away. My arm hurt more and more although all the doctors said it was fine and mended well. It was strange, I enjoyed my work, reading Plato and Hume and Heidegger. I think they make sense. It was because my work was so good that it took them so long to realise that there was something wrong with me. It got so that I couldn't move my arm and I couldn't write. It was only because I didn't give in essays for a while that they noticed. Then my mother came to get me and take me home. After a while they took me to hospital. It was funny, my father was as nice as he could be. Once he knew there was a real reason for me being like I was, it was O.K. Something positive to tell his banking friends.

Once they left me in that place, I forgot about my parents. They came to see me a few times, but I'd only look at them to check that my descriptions were right. Gordon never came and I'm glad. I didn't want to see him. All I know is that he's been in hospital a few times, because people beat him up. But I think he still thinks he's right. Sometimes I wonder if he is, but I think that's only because I used to love him so much. I think I know he's not. I was there for a few years. You get used to it after a while. Well, I suppose you never get used to it, but it's surprising how little you hate it by the end. Now I realise that my doctor wasn't all bad, I just think he was a bit misguided. Because however often I think of Gordon and his black shirt, it never gets any better.

It was my doctor who got me this job with the laundry. Which was nice of him I suppose. When I first started it I had to go back to the hospital every night. But now I have my rooms, that I walk around all the time. I have to take pills, but not as many as before. And, like I said, I'm glad to have another day usually. The nights that I get my attacks get further and further apart, which is another good sign. Sometimes I get upset about my job and things. As though it's not enough or something. But I have more than some people, I mean those people I left behind in the hospital. But I don't want to start all that over again. That's why I sit at my kitchen bar and think about things. It's like I'm just checking to make sure no one has realised what I am, or what I'd like to do. I like looking at women and thinking about them, but I know that if I actually talked to any of them my arm would start to hurt again.

Strange, the other day I was sitting in my kitchen, smoking my cigarette and I remembered something my father shouted at my mother that night as I lay on the floor with my broken arm. He shouted, 'Penelope's always been the runt. She's always been strange. Pen, the runt.' It's funny that: Pen the runt.

Like I say, I have my good days. Maybe when I start having more good days next to each other, I'll break out of this man-made pen of mine.

The Party Game

A hesitancy, a hush: Click-swing and there he stands. In the doorway. What is he looking at? Standing behind her? She turns at last, to see just what it is. It is her – he looks at her.

'Well, is everything ready?' he asks.

'What do you mean?'

'For tonight. Is everything ready?'

'Oh yes. I've done everything I can think of. You'll have to drive down to the off licence to buy the booze. Apart from that I've done everything. How many do you reckon will come?'

'Oh, I don't know. Sixty, seventy. Maybe less. I'm going to have a bath, O.K.? I won't be long.'

She turns and looks in the mirror, unseeing, swaying a little. What will it be like, this evening? Will she enjoy herself? Will anyone enjoy the evening? Grimacing at the face that looks back at her, she reaches for her hair brush.

'Have you got the lemons? Do you remember, I asked you to get lots of lemons?'

A cry from the bathroom. A cry from the soul? She feels her throat rasp as tears rush through her body, then she hardens before her own eyes.

'Oh damn. No. Sorry, I forgot.'

'What?' Paddy-bare-footsteps. He stands in a doorway again. 'You didn't get any? Where the hell can I buy lemons now?'

'The supermarket will still be open when you get the booze. You could get them then. I'm sorry, I just forgot, I had so much to buy. Food and everything.'

'But you've had all week to sort everything out. I've been working all week, and I'm still expected to arrange it all.' He frowns.

'It's only a few lemons. Why don't you have your bath? The water must be running over.'

'Oh Christ!' He turns and runs to the bathroom, his buttocks young and shaking. Steam snakes out into the bedroom, touching her as she watches him.

'You'd better get ready now, in case anyone comes early. What're you going to wear?' yells Mr Misty-Voice, through the closed door.

'Surely no one will come now? It's only half-past six. No one ever seems to come before midnight.'

'What?'

'The black thing.' Raising her voice. 'Oh God.' Muttering.

She waits in the middle of the spacious bedroom, sunk in the deep pile of the dark grey carpet. The hours leer in front of her as she realises that she will not get to bed until early morning. The sound of splashing and slurping as the water rollicks in the bath.

'Do you want to scrub my back?' his voice cries.

'No. No, I don't want to.'

'Oh go on.'

'No.'

She puts on a red dress and sits, once more, in front of the mirror. Her face is an expressionless mask as she applies the mask of make-up that she is expected to wear tonight. Her husband walks though from the bathroom as she is painting on a new lip line. His wet, flat feet leave damp, dark, crushed carpet behind him.

'Why don't you wear your black dress? It's sexy.'

'Because I don't want to be sexy.'

'Well you are. Even in that thing.'

'What's wrong with it?'

'Nothing. It's just old, that's all. Why do you have so many clothes when you wear the old ones all the time?'

'They were all new at some time or another.'

Giving her a pitying smile in the mirror he leans over her shoulder to comb his wet hair.

'I shall have to hurry, Roger said he might come straight after work, so he may be here at any moment.' He says this squinting at his parting. 'Works in publicity. You'll like him.'

'Oh.'

'Where's my burgundy jumper? Do you know?'

'You're holding it.'

'No, not this one. I don't like it. The other one.'

'That's the only clean one.'

'Oh, balls. It's not is it?'

'Yes, I thought you meant me to wash that one.'

'Damn. I'll have to wear another.'

'Yes.'

'Did anyone call today? I mean, to say they weren't coming?'

'Yes. But it was only the Bests, so it doesn't really matter, does it? They said they were very sorry, but their kid's ill. They offered to come over some other time.'

'Oh, right.'

Turning from the mirror he unwraps the towel around his hips. Naked, he walks to the wardrobe and flicks through his clothes as through a book. His wife cannot shatter his nerves: he is a thunderball of anticipation. He hears her shifting on her chair behind him. Feels her brown eyes raking his back.

'You know you said that you were going to invite Ruth and Melanie, you didn't mean it, did you?' she asks, as he knew she would.

'Do you think I should wear a tie?'

'Did you? Have you invited them?'

'What's the time?'

'Seven o'clock. You have, haven't you? You've invited them.'

'Of course I have. Ruth's a designer for the firm, I see her every day. She'd heard all about tonight, so I had to invite her. It would have looked funny if I hadn't.'

'You could have asked her if she'd come without Melanie. Did you? Ask her I mean?'

'No, of couse I didn't. I said that she and Melanie were both welcome to come. Does this look alright?'

The young woman stands up, pushing her hands against her knees, and walks out of the bedroom, into the kitchen. There are plates piled with food, lines of sparkling, thin-stemmed wine glasses, rows of cardboard-contained fruit juices, covering every surface of the room. Otherwise it is bare, as is the rest of the flat. All pictures, ornaments, books, china, paper, tables have been taken out and put in the garage. Looking around she feels as if she had just moved into the flat, and is waiting for the furniture van to arrive. Waiting to start a new life.

'Well, does it look alright?'

'What?'

'The jumper.'

He has followed her, and stands in front of her smiling.

'Oh yes. It looks just wonderful.'

'I thought so,' he says, still smiling.

'I don't think you should have invited them.'

'Who? Ruth and Melanie? Why on earth not? You're obsessed with them.'

'It's just that they'll look out of place. They're not normal.'

'What do you mean, "not normal"? Just because they sleep together? Which is none of our business.'

'I'm sure that you don't like them particularly, it's just that you want to appear liberal. I don't know.'

'I do happen to like them. Ruth is one of my best friends.'

'Crap.'

'Look, let's not let this ruin everything.'

'Everything? What do you mean? Ruin the evening? Oh, no, you're not going to pretend that you're actually looking forward to this hellish party?' She feels the tears returning and looks away from the man in front of her.

'Yes I am,' he says.

'Well it's more than I am.'

He walks into the small bar that is their kitchen and pours himself a small drink. Glancing through the window in the end wall he sees Roger parking his car and reaching for a bottle on the back seat. His mood is beginning to crack; he must leave his wife soon, to fetch the drink and lemons. He looks back to his wife.

'You're not looking forward to it because they're coming. Ruth and Melanie. No, it's not even that. It's because most of the people I've invited are from the office, isn't it? That's why you didn't invite any of your intellectual friends.'

'What are you talking about? I don't understand what you're talking about. What's that got to do with Ruth and Melanie?'

'I think you like them as much as I do, it's just that you don't know where to put them. I refuse to let you spoil this evening, so I'm not going to talk about this anymore. Just stop worrying about stupid things.'

The couple stare at each other, unspeaking across the divide of the kitchen. Stupid things? What is he saying? Still she does not understand. But then, neither does he. Ruth and Melanie are not the point, exactly. She does like them, but that is not the point. What to do with them? Pretend they are the same as everyone else? Ignore the thing that makes them different? Just where *should* she put them in her scheme of things? It's alright for him. He treats them as he would any woman, leering politely over his glass. Is that what he thinks she should do? She frowns at the man who stands smiling distantly at her. A bell rings.

'That'll be Roger and I haven't even been to the off licence. Look, can you talk to him whilst I go into town? He'll have brought something so give him that to drink. I won't be long.' He kisses her as he walks past.

The husband and the drink have returned. The room is full, people have spilled out into the garden. Smoke floats in a wavering field above her head. The noise continues as it has for hours. She had been right: they had all arrived late, full of wine and food, all shouting and screaming. Cries of recognition and delight each time the door opens. She had been wrong: everyone enjoys the party, except her. Roger had been awful, and she had had him to herself for over an hour. Since then, all the people she had talked to had been drunk. But, more than that, Ruth and Melanie have not arrived, and now she realises that she would enjoy talking to them. She is still shocked by her husband's speech. Perhaps he is right? Ruth and Melanie did seem to get on very well. They never embarrassed her by touching each other in front of everyone, in fact they hardly seemed to be a couple at all. It was just that there were looks and smiles that made you realise, that excluded you in the gentlest way possible. And now she was standing here, alone. No-one wanted to talk to her, they were all shouting about their work, their firm, their department. But what could she talk about? What was that film she had seen? Recently, on television. A young woman sitting in a room, watching, listening, not sure if those talking around her were remarkably brilliant or remarkably stupid. 'The Lacemaker', that was it. Black and white, French. Urchin film. Laden with angst and Gauloises. The smoke in the room is thickening even more. She moves to the window and opens it. Outside, in a car parked in the road, are Ruth and Melanie. She stands watching, with her hand on the window, pressed on the glass. Frozen.

In the car, as at the party, the smoke hangs heavy. Neither woman speaks. A cyclist passes the car and they both watch until he turns a corner. Ruth slowly lowers her head to the rim of the steering wheel and sighs. Her thick coat is pulled tightly round her, the collar standing up around her neck and hiding most of her face. It is cold and she rubs her hands. The woman next to her opens a small window to throw out the butt of her cigarette, closing the window quickly. She stuffs her hands in the arms of her jumper. She is younger than Ruth and she is crying. Silent, snotty crying that shakes her body and rocks the car slightly. Melanie raises her muffled hands and wipes her nose on the wrists of her jumper. Sniffing she turns to look at the profile of the older woman, silhouetted against the street light. She stares at her, uncomprehending and then lets her head fall against the window on her side of the car.

'Nice time to tell me,' she murmurs.

'What would you rather I had done? Waited for a while? Gone on pretending?'

'Yes. Of course.'

'Don't be daft, what good would that have done?' Ruth lifts her head to gaze out of the windscreen. She cannot look at the desperate bundle beside her. 'I couldn't go on pretending. I've been leading a double life for months. Dashing between you and her. It's worn me out.'

'You want my sympathy? My God. And don't mention her again or I'll get out and go.' The young woman has sat up and is shouting.

'O.K. I'm sorry. Look, it's not the end of everything. We can still see each other. We've been together for too long to just walk away.'

All night, Melanie thinks, all night she has been doing this, as we sit in this car. She has been fighting and cooing. Aggression and triteness in equal measure. All night sitting in this bloody car. Aggressive because she is filled with self-disgust, trite because she has no imagination. She wants me to leave or to go into that bloody party and behave normally, anything but this.

'Melanie, look, I think we should go into David and Lesley's and have a drink and talk to some people, try to calm down. It would help both of us.'

'You want us to go in there and pretend that nothing's happened, and on top of that, pretend that we're not together as usual? Not to talk to each other, fend off the usual lechers with a smile? Jesus. You've no idea of what you've done to me. I love you and you want to leave me. And now you want me to be happy and go on playing the same games? Ruth, do you know how much that hurts me? That little party game of appearances. How much it wears me out.'

'You think it doesn't hurt me too?'

There she goes again, pulling at my emotional collar, pulling me here and there, across the whole emotional map. Playing with my love like a practiced angler playing with a boisterous trout. Melanie presses her head to the glass and weeps.

'Oh, my God,' she gasps. 'I'm dying. I can't bear it. Don't make me go in there. Stop hurting me and take me away.'

'Look honey, I've got to show my face. I said we'd both go. David asked both of us. It'll be fine. He likes you.'

'Why don't you?'

'I do. Of course I do. I love you. That's why I want you to come. It will help.'

'You just want to disperse my unhappiness so far that you won't be able to see it anymore. Oh God, it hurts.' Melanie's mouth opens and a cry emerges. A cry that fills the car. She slumps across the seat and pushes her face into the other woman's thick, homey coat, shaking with misery, twisting the wool between her fingers. She is home. This is home. This coat that Ruth wears all winter, that hangs on the bannisters. That will soon be gone. The older woman stares ahead, rubbing her forehead with her fingers. She cannot touch the helpless girl. It has passed. She started something that cannot stop. That will stop if she touches Melanie. It is over. She can do nothing. The cry wails on, muffled, unceasing.

'Take me home. Take me away. Take me home. Take me away.'

Ruth leans over the heaving back and turns the ignition key. Looking at the house one last time she notices a woman staring at the car, a woman who has been there some time. The woman is leaning against nothing, or so it seems. Gently moving the girl's head onto her shoulder, Ruth puts the car into gear and moves away from the house, glaring dry-eyed at the road ahead.

Lesley, still touching the glass, leans through the

window, away from the crowded room, and watches the car disappear. Misunderstanding, always misunderstanding, she cries softly after it.

'Take me with you. Please. Take me with you.'

Avocadoes for Breakfast

It is the morning and I lie here awake at last. As I stare ceiling-wards I feel something small and woolly nudging me, herding me towards an acknowledgement of something. I am resisting, fighting for a few more innocent moments. But the wooliness is winning, as always, shoving me with its blunt, unfeeling nose. The picture it is forcing me to see blurs and then sharpens. I look elsewhere. The climbing plant in the corner: crawling each hour towards the window that I shall never open for it. Crawling and climbing for days, stretching its tendrils hopelessly towards the light. As you did with your arms, mistaking me for the light. At the end of the bed there is a bundle of clothes that must be mine, although I can't tell in this curtain-drawn twilight that I have created. Their colours are blank; dead-blues and greys.

There are noises below me, and I have reached the moment when I must turn and look at the sharpened picture in its entirety. You are here, downstairs, making noises in the kitchen. If only I had woken earlier, to armour myself. Against what? Myself, for I am the enemy. Please stay down there whilst I pull the curtains and leave this room to splash water on my face. Please leave me alone for that small, short time. Stay in my kitchen, you can stay there forever, if you'd let me leave without seeing you this morning. I don't want to think of you down there, moving amongst the things that are all mine, moving in my house. I don't want to think of you in one of my shirts, walking the same worn, pale blue path as I have from sink to kettle. I don't want to think of the kettle making the same noises for you as for me. If I think of it, I'll be able to imagine your feet on the hard floor. I would like to think of you padding through piled carpets, walking on silks, velvet floor-ways, cushioning yourself against anything that might happen, anything that I might do. The letter box bangs and I know that you are standing in the hallway, not knowing whether to pick up the envelopes and carry them back to the kitchen. Please don't. Leave them lying as they are so that I can come down to find them; they are mine.

I turn on the taps to hide the sound of my not-breathing. I can feel the flimsy curtains of moments floating down from ceiling to floor as I stand here wondering how to speak to you. Each moment that I stay up here, away from you, makes my walking down the stairs more difficult, having to brush aside those curtains.

Why won't you leave? Walk out now, leaving me to stand untouched in my bathroom. Walk out and away to where you live, away to your own kitchen. Why didn't you just get up and leave, pass through the front door and on to the street, where I cannot find you? Is it because you know that I wouldn't try to? Is it because you feel I must now pay, here, this morning? Are you looking through the window at those things I look at every morning, cloaked in sunshine and waiting for the sound of my steps on the stairs? What can I say that will make you feel any better, or is it that you don't care about feeling better? Is it that you want to see me as you have never seen me before: unloving and remorseful? So that you can carry that memory of me with you when you do finally walk out?

My steps on the stairs sound strange to me, just as I am trying to make them sound as they do every morning for your benefit. Or my own. I pick up my letters and stand in the hall opening them, delaying the moment. It has to be now, I must walk into the kitchen. Your back is turned, I can't tell if you have heard me. You're looking out of the window and don't turn to look at me. It is more than I had hoped for: another moment.

'Hello.'

'Oh, hello.'

You have turned at last, startled. You had not heard me, and I find I'm surprised.

'How are you? Did you sleep alright? Were you making coffee?'

'Yes, do you want some?'

'It's O.K., I'll get it.'

You're wearing one of my shirts, but not the one that I had imagined. I must have pictured you with greater clarity than I'd thought. Right down to your feet.

'Did you ... Did you sleep alright?'

'Yes, thanks. It's a lovely room.'

'Mmm, it is, isn't it? I did it up last year. I always wanted a study, so I thought I'd change it. It's worked out O.K. ...'

'Yes, it has.'

'Would you like some more coffee, or do you still ... do you prefer tea?'

'No, coffee's fine. Black, please.'

'Would you like something to eat? I've got all the usual stuff. I could cook you something. Or do you just want toast? Whatever you want. I've, um, I've got some avocadoes if you'd like one. They're great in the morning. You know, just on their own.'

'I've never had one in the morning.'

'Go on, try one, they're great.'

'Alright.'

'I'll get some. They're up in the bathroom so they can ripen. Won't be a minute.'

This is much better than I thought it would be. Perhaps I won't have to say anything after all. You're being wonderful, acting as if nothing had happened. Perhaps you're not acting; perhaps you don't mind and I've made the mistake of thinking that you did. But surely last night mattered a bit? Not much, but a little? I'm not saying anything unless you do. It's not my place to, it's yours. Maybe you thought of leaving and just didn't have the time.

'Here they are, they're ready, really soft.'

'You don't have anything with them?'

'No, unless you want some yoghurt.'

'No, no, this is fine.'

'Do you want anything to drink?'

'I never want to drink again after last night.'

'No, I mean orange juice or something like that. I could squeeze some fresh.'

'Yes, please ... You've got everything haven't you? Well set up.'

It's coming. I should have offered you nothing. I should have let you go as you wanted to last night. I should have stayed upstairs. I should have been born a better person.

'These are delicious. I'd never have thought of having them for breakfast before. Why did you ask me back last night?'

'I don't know.'

'I was happy, you know, not knowing where you lived, or how you lived. Not being able to picture it. Oh, I knew that you lived in London but I didn't know where, and you can't imagine anything at all if you don't even know where someone lives. What sort of work do you do?'

'I told you last night. I work for a publisher.'

'Oh yes, of course. I forgot. I was very drunk.'

'Yes, so was I.'

'Is that your excuse? For asking me back?'

'No, no. Of course not. I just thought that since we were getting on so well ...'

'Aren't you going to eat yours?' Cause if not, I'll have it.'

Yes, you have it. You can have everything, if only you'd go. I don't have any excuses. But you could have made it easier for me, instead of sitting there in my shirt, eating breakfast with me. It's just as we planned it all those years ago. You and me sitting down to our breakfast in a sunlit kitchen. And I can't ask you to leave, and you know it. So, I'll sit it out, listen to whatever you have to say, because sooner or later you'll have to go. You know that, and that's why you're being so cruel.

'Thank you. You were saying?'

'Yes, well, I mean, we haven't seen each other for ages and when we met last night I was pleased to see you, really I was. And we got on so well that it seemed a pity to stop, so I thought it would be a good idea if ... well ... if we came back here ... I don't know. I was drunk.'

'Go on.'

'That's it. I can't think of anything else to say.'

'Do you really want to know what I think was sick about last night? Do you? It's the fact that, after rolling around on the floor with me and talking to me as you did, you were too scared to let me sleep with you. I had to sleep in another room. I expect that you were hoping that I'd get up and go, without seeing you. Well, I've been up for hours, since before dawn, sitting down here thinking about whether to go or to wait for you to wake up, and I decided to stay. Because I think you should know what I thought of you and what I think of you now.'

'I don't want to hear. I'm sorry for last night and for all those things I said. I wasn't as drunk as I'm trying to make out, and I can remember them. I shouldn't have said them, although I sort of meant them at the time. But you know as well as I do that we can't be as we were. We've both changed so much since then. I don't know you. I was just thinking about the past and how it was, and it was wonderful. I just got carried away by an idea and the drink. I apologise.'

'And now I'm supposed to go? Is that it? Don't worry, I shall in a while. Not long. I just want you to know that I was happy until last night, when I saw you. Oh, yes, I was happy all evening, just sitting and talking to you. But you should never have said those things. I know they were transparently false, but I can still hear you saying them. And now I'll wonder, I'll be able to imagine all the things that you do. What you'll be doing in this house. Where you sleep, where you eat. What your room looks like. The picture that I had of you had faded completely. It really had. I heard from other people that you had changed, that you looked different, and so you do. But now I have a fresh picture and I'll be able to see you, as you are now, doing things. Before it was like sepia or something. You know those photos of us in Greece? I tore them up years ago. So I wouldn't be able to look at them and remember what you look like. And when people said you'd changed, God, was I pleased, because I couldn't fit all the ways they described you into the person I knew. Now I can and it's terrible. I wish I didn't know.'

'Look, I didn't go into that pub on purpose. I didn't know that you'd be in there. How could I?'

'I know that. You don't have to tell me that. The funny thing is that I spent so much of my time trying to find you after we'd finished. I'd hear that you were working in Holborn, South Ken, anywhere, and I'd make excuses to go drinking there. I'd take other people along, as a sort of cover. Then gradually I stopped doing that. That's when I destroyed your photographs. And I forgot, very slowly, but I did forget. It took ages. I was happy, for the first time in years. For the first time since I last saw you. Do you remember that time? God, I was so angry with you.'

You've got to say these things, I know, and I must listen. But I must not care. I must not show you that I care. I never meant to hurt you twice, but I can't even tell you that. Unloving and remorseful.

'The point is ... and I've thought of it a lot since then ... the point is that you didn't even care that I was angry and crying, did you? You didn't even care enough to try to wonder why. Well, this morning I decided to stay, to wait for you, because I know that you'll have to listen to me, for a while at least, because you haven't got the guts to throw me out, as you want to. Don't bother to argue with me, I know that it's true. I just want you to know that I never understood why you left me and that's why I was so unhappy for so long. You never explained, you just left. I never understood and that's why it hurt so much. You didn't even care enough to explain. After all that time and all that we'd said, you couldn't even tell me why. And I could see in you a fear. The fear that I wouldn't go away, that I'd hound you forever. Well, don't worry, I won't. I was happy and would still have been happy if I'd never seen you. But I have.'

'Look, if you want me to tell you why ...'

'Let me finish and then I'll go. Last night, when I saw you, I thought it didn't matter that you never explained, that it was something I should never have worried about. I don't know why, but I did. But now I can still hear all those things that you said back here, and I know that it will take me months, even years, all over again, to forget that you said them, to not wonder if you meant them. And now I know that it does matter that you didn't tell me why, and the funny thing is that now I know why. I've guessed your reasons for leaving me. They're so shallow I won't even ask you if I'm right. You've done this to me before, so I know all about it. And I don't want you to say anything.'

You're leaving me to carry on as I have always done, leaving me to my swift loss of guilt. I find that I'm sorry, not for not explaining or for saying those things last night, but because you are here at all.

Spit in the Desert

I

Have I done the right thing? I have left everything in order to start a new life elsewhere, not knowing what is there for me. I must fashion it from raw materials that will feel strange to the touch. That will feel strange to my touch. I have not thought of what this life may be, I have not thought of the degree of change. Abandoning things can be this easy – should not be this easy. I have walked away from my friends, my home, my work. I have abandoned the ship of London life. Grimy London–life that weaves around all who live there its web of expectation, responsibility and avarice. Oh, but it is easy to leave, to unweave that web: I have just done it. Was it that I did not dare to think? I have spent months saving money, working whenever possible, building brick-by-brick a dam of money which will protect me, cushion me. Against what? Against what will I need protection? What is it that has stepped forward and now hovers at the corner of my mind's eye? Until this morning nothing had come to me, to question what I was doing. I thought only of reaching the airport, reaching my goal of the past months. This date, twenty-eighth December, has been my goal for so long that, now it is here, I no longer know what to do. Be happy. Be happy. She will be there and things will fall into place. It will be as I have imagined. She will be standing there and I will walk through those doors and we will almost crash into each other; these doubts will shatter and the pieces will fall into place around us. A mosaic of hope will build itself as we stand entwined in that hall, as I remember what it is to hold someone I love more than anyone. Why, then, do I feel small nuggets of fear breaking all through my body? Pins of doubt pricking my dehydrating skin.

When I walked through the door of this plane, a trap shut, and another door opened that will lead me through a drama I shall not want to play. Looking out of the window I see only the fields of clouds that seem to buoy the plane as it flies towards the sun. Endless white billowing cloud, there is nothing else to watch. I am in a shroud, I cannot see anything except myself and these clouds. I am flying to New England. I must believe that I am flying to a new England, for I have left the old one.

I have half an hour to compose myself, before her plane lands. Thirty minutes to examine the future, when a moment should be enough. When I know that thirty minutes will not be enough. What will happen? I have had no time to think. How has this happened? How has this thing crept in? Four months ago I landed here, at this airport, awash with tears, missing her so much I thought I would die. As I stepped out into this airport, the heat of dying summer nearly flattened me and yet still I felt cold. Brimming with cold fear: fear of what was coming, fear that I had made a mistake in leaving her. Now I can't even remember her clearly, I don't know her. Now I can't even remember myself as I was, my London-self. I know only my Boston-self, my American-self. But why think of this now? I have had months to think, to imagine. Believing it would be alright, on this day, believing that when I see her the other will be washed away. Believing that when I see her I shall become my old self again, that the months we have been apart will fade and discolour, crumble to dust. Now I am not sure.

I should be on the verge of happiness, but instead I am imagining another place: the place where Vivienne is for the next week. Washington made more beautiful by Vivienne being there. I should be here in this airport, focusing on that door, waiting for Julia to walk through. But instead I watch imagining Vivienne walking through in a burst of colour, smiling, sweeping me away. It will not be Vivienne, it will be my lover, the woman I have loved for what seems forever. And yet it is not forever. It has not been long, perhaps not long enough. This day was to have been the happiest of the months I have spent here. Instead, I stand here full of fear again.

Perhaps it will be alright? Perhaps she will walk through and be enough. Enough for what? Where can I put her in my new life? There's no room for her. She comes here with nothing but money, expecting me to accommodate her, to move over and let her in, to build another life for her. But, if I won't do it, who will? I have let her come, I have encouraged her to come, I have told her that I love her still. Perhaps I do? When I see her, perhaps, the illusion of this life will fade and she will make things as they were before. Before what? Before Vivienne.

The plane is in. The waiting is over. She is here in this building. Will my enchantment last, or will my fantasy be dispelled with a look? To be replaced by another enchantment? God help me if I find that I have done wrong in letting her come here. Was it only last night that I spoke to Vivienne? Only the day before that, that we lay in bed, silent, each wondering what to do with our old loves and our new-found love? I am scared, as the moment approaches. I need you, Vivienne, I need you to tell me what to do ... She is here, behind those doors. The hands of the clock are turning and I can't stop them. Still I am not ready, but I know I shall never be ready for this. I never thought of this. That I would actually see her here, in Vivienne-Land. Yet it was I who said she should come. How did this happen? What can I do when I am *so scared? Please let her be enough, please let her walk through and be enough. I need more time, I haven't thought, I can't compose myself.*

The door is opening and people are walking out. Her flight has definitely come in. Where is she? Now the time has come I want to see her, I want to know. There. There she is. She looks no different. She turns and sees me. It is her, the person I wanted more than anyone, she is with me, she has come to me. But nothing has changed, Vivienne. Nothing is shattered.

She is waiting as I knew she would be. Smiling and waving. Wait, wait, I must gather up my bags. Walk through the door, gateway to what? I am here at last, I am here with my hopes and my love. Hugging her as though it were yesterday I last saw her. Remembering her body, the smell of her, the feel of her. I am tired and hungry, yet I could stand here forever, holding her. As though it were yesterday? But it was not yesterday, it has been months. I look at her and the thing hovering at the corner of my mind's eye hops nearer. Still I cannot focus on it. Something is wrong. This is not as it should be. We cannot look at each other, smiling. Perhaps it is the months themselves that stand between us? I want to get out of the airport.

Not so bad, not so bad. Now that we are away from that place and riding through Boston, through the streets I know and past places I have been, it is not so bad. She looks tired, strained, but her hand feels the same as before as it lies in my hand. The picture of her is clearing as I watch her sitting with her head thrown back, eyes closed. I can remember things we have done, I can remember when we have been happy. Maybe it will be alright; she is more than I remembered. I can feel the bulk of her from here: the laugh, the anger, the stories. I have thought of her as a chameleon, but I can see now that she does not change, that she has not changed. But it was not her changing that I wondered about. What can I give her?

She always seemed to have so much more than me, now she has nothing but me. But there is no time left to think. She is here, and our life has ground into motion. Perhaps she will be enough?

The sun is blinding and yet there are mounds of dirty snow on the road, on roofs, on cars. Sun and snow? Something I have not seen for years. The cars are huge, lumbering around these roads. Yet I can see small cars, weaving around the monsters. Another difference I had not anticipated. The houses covered in wood, all painted different colours, just like the pictures. Strange sounds: horns and sirens and American voices on the car radio. The taxi driver in lumberjack shirt and flat-cap, growling at other drivers.

How long is it since I slept? Last night, however long ago that was, I lay in bed trying to think of how I would be doing this that I am now doing. Strange, how every time I leave England I think I'll be different when I arrive elsewhere, but of course I'm still the same. It is still me sitting here, my eyes closed, listening. It is still my hand, with all the same nicks, cuts and scars that holds hers as we drive to our home of the next month. I have travelled thousands of miles to be here and I can't think of anything to say to her. It is the tiredness, the shock of finally being where I did not think I could ever be. Yet it is the only afternoon, I can't sleep now. It is only the tiredness, the loneliness of the just-arrived, it can't be anything else. Oh I know I'm talking, talking about all these things I can see (the alien, glittering skyline piercing something within me with its malignant spires) but I'm not saying anything. Why can't I turn and freeze her with my love, saying, 'I am moved by you as I have been by no one else. I have always been there for you, I have always wanted to shelter you from things that might harm you. I love you. Will you bear with me? Will you, now, in turn, shelter me? Keep me safe?'

I can tell that she is dazed, and becoming more so, by things that I see as normal, accept as normal. I tell the driver, 'The corner of Magazine and Auburn', and she is amazed. She doesn't even know where she is. As the cab stops she looks around, unseeing. What can I show her?

As we struggle up the stairs with the luggage, my heart holds its breath. She has so much, so many bags. Of course she would have this much; she is not here for a holiday. But she is weighed down with it and it doesn't suit her. She should be weighed down only with stories, anger and laughter, wild nights and vivid language. How could she pack all those things in these bags, already sagging? I am holding her life in my hands and dropping it. I turn to see her staring at me strangely – or perhaps she always did? Why can't I remember her properly? I know that this is important, perhaps the most important thing that has happened to me, so why can't I think of it. I'm only half here and the rest of me buzzes around the honey-pot notion of Washington–Vivienne. My emotions are flexing and moving, bird-like they dart from one idea to another, never settling. But I must not show her that this is happening to me.

I watch her as she sits slumped in a chair talking about our friends in London, nursing a can of beer, smoking cigarette after cigarette, and I am moved by her. There is a stirring within me of the old love. She tells me her stories, and they are funny, they touch a nerve, a nerve that has been dormant since I last saw her (how long ago?). Now I realise that she is not exactly the same as I left her: She has done things and been with people I don't even know, she has got drunk and argued, travelled around, visited clubs and pubs. She has, in short, lived her life, but running always on the same rails.

And me? What have I done? I could not run along the same lines, I have been in a different country, amongst different people. She tells me about those people we both know. What can I tell her about? I find myself mentioning Vivienne, talking about the things we have done together, because it is she that fills my life. I talk about her or I sit in silence. The evening rolls on and slowly my heart draws breath, but still it does not know which way to jump. I begin to love her more as I remember more. But I know I have not opened my doors to her, flung them open and let her crawl in. I still watch from a distance, distanced by other things. Yet, strangely, we are touching as we always did, hands brushing, knees bumping, small kisses exchanged as small flares. And it doesn't feel wrong. I can't imagine being with her and not touching, as though we each use the power-house of the other to charge ourselves for the next slice of time.

But although I am waking, slowly, to the possibility of her, there is something missing and I worry that it has gone forever. I can't recall how it must have been before, when we would spend whole days in bed, when a touch from her would send lust flashing through me. But, what can I do? I cannot tell her, for I am still not sure. Perhaps she will be enough. Perhaps, once in bed, I will reawaken to her. We have swapped stories of our entanglements with others whilst we have been apart, yet her stories are throwaway. While for me something has shifted. I feel for Vivienne what I have felt for her. Oh, Julia, what have I done? I still love you so much. What might I have done to you? I wish I could talk to you about it, you would know what to do.

It was wonderful and deathly at the same time. The feel of her skin and the contours of her body; to hear her breathing next to me is almost an elixir. The sense of belonging again, at last, nearly overwhelms me but not quite, not quite. For behind the moments that have just passed, behind all the oil-slick, sweat-oiled movements, flits a shadow. Shadowing each move that I make is a question: is that what you do with her? With Vivienne? Kathy, my Kathy, lies next to me curled in the very shape of a question mark, marking my future and my present. She sleeps as I lie here, rigid, unable to stop thinking. My insides freeze and thaw in a state of flux as, unasked, a thought repeats itself. What am I doing here? Already I am an island. I cannot wake her and say, 'Hold me I'm scared. Do you want me?' How can she sleep when I can't? She should be here for me, as I fall apart. What is that phrase, the phrase that is brushing against my mind? 'I came to see you minded.' Surely not – it's too far to come to see if someone does something as genteel as minding.

II

A week has passed since I first saw this snow. Even here, on the balcony, looking out over Boston, it's underfoot. Cracking and squeaking. And it's so cold, below freezing, I can't get used to it. But it's better than being in the flat, squashed with fake heat, shut in by glass two panes thick. The room Kathy and I have been staying in, the room that is supposed to be stopgap whilst we find somewhere else in which to lead our life, is driving me mad. I know every inch of it, I have lain on the bed watching the light change as the day wallows and dies on the snow outside. The sounds I can hear are still strange, the shops still confuse me. I know I'm not sinking into this place, I think of myself as a splinter under a nail. Wedged and aching; but no one has the guts to ease me out, to prise me loose. Least of all, Kathy. And I can't tell where the shock of the new ends and the sense of impending loss begins. For there is a sense of loss: I am losing Kathy, inch by shuddering inch, as though I'm holding her wrist as she dangles over a precipice and she is slipping, slipping, only to fall into Vivienne's arms.

Snow is starting to drift again, frosting the wooden, cube-like house with a brittle, flashing veneer. No, it is not falling, it is being blown by a wind that has something called a chill factor. However they bundle up this cold in words, it still saws through me. What do people think as they pass by, looking up to see me leaning on a snow-strewn rail, looking out over this beautiful city, smoking cigarettes?

I know the skyline so well now, I could draw it in my sleep. Boston – I may know the city from a distance, but I have not trodden its streets, peered into its shops, visited its bars. I dare not. What is the point of becoming attached to this place, if all I will do is say another goodbye?

Somewhere out in those streets Kathy is walking, coming home from work. Well, not home; this flat will never be home. That room will never welcome either of us. At least I know she is coming home from her work, today being the last time I shall be sure of that, for tomorrow things will change. Vivienne and Gabrielle fly into Boston tomorrow morning, and from that moment I shall never be sure where Kathy is. But then, they can't see each other, except with stealth, for Gabrielle is here for two more weeks. Has Vivienne told her, warned her off, apologised? So many questions I can't ask, since I won't believe any of the answers. Kathy can't even lie properly, let alone tell the truth. She really doesn't think I know about the danger and extent of her love for Vivienne.

Poor Gabrielle, she came all the way from Amsterdam for this. I feel for both of us, but at least Gabrielle is only here for a few weeks. She has not thrown everything away. Perhaps she and I will be thrown away? God, it's so cold. Across the river the sun glints off the mirror towers, flashes on windscreens, slithers along the frozen river. Does Kathy imagine that I can imagine nothing? Does she think that I don't notice her flinch every time the phone rings?

Can it really only be a week, seven days and nights, that I have been here? Only six days since we sat in a coffee shop in Harvard Square, the morning after that deathless first night? Kathy had still said nothing, had transformed her guilt into an ungainly jollity. Even then, I loved her so much I wanted to make it easier for her.

'So, what's all this about Vivienne? Is she in love with you?'

'Yes.'

'Are you in love with her?'

'Yes.'

'Oh.'

'But I still love you.'

That's all it was. But even then I had to say it, she

couldn't. Would she have told me if I hadn't asked? What would have happened? No point, none, in thinking of it. And then that New Year's Eve party, with me still tired from the journey, tired from so much thinking. Hugging her at midnight, unable to look into her eyes, in case she, too, was thinking of the evening a year before, in a loud, beery pub in London, surrounded by friends, who cheered as we kissed each other. Such awkwardness, awkwardness everywhere. This New Year's Eve I felt I was surrounded, if not by enemies, then by people who did not know what to do with me, for they had watched Kathy and Vivienne at other parties. I think back, and imagine her standing in a room, holding the phone, listening to my excitement, unable to spit out what must have been trembling on the edge of her answers. All the people at that bloody New Year party knew, only I hadn't been told. I feel like a leper.

But I'm not going to fight this. Indeed, I'm not sure how I could, because no one will acknowledge that there is a battle raging somewhere. We three English women playing out an understated drama in a land that does not lend itself to understatement. In front of people who look on with interest. I know you can't make someone love you. I tried once before, years ago, so now I'm at least armed with that knowledge. A flimsy shield, really. And yet I know that Kathy isn't thinking, 'How could I have loved her? Loved Julia?' No. She seems to be trying to work out how she can stop loving me.

So many mornings I have woken to find Kathy watching me, having watched me as I sleep. My vulnerability stretched even further. Each morning, looking in the mirror, I find a worried, dimensionless face looking back. A face flattened with fear. If I were a man, I'd look unshaven; but women implode, their pain is more difficult to see. Yet I know that Kathy can see mine. And I've noticed my eyelids are red and swollen each morning, with the lashes jammed deep in them. I must cry in my sleep. I dare not cry at any other time for it would make this worse, would make Kathy crack. Yes, I look dreadful. I'm not fighting. I'm not forcing anything. How can I? I'm a ridiculous enough figure as it is. But a part of me feels that this is right: I am unimportant. I am not the point, merely the point around which this struggle revolves. In short, I am dispensable. I feel I should leave, but there is nowhere to go, and I may still have Kathy, although that becomes harder and harder to believe.

Even colder now, as the sun moves away, the shadows a deep, bloodless blue against the snow. Wind ruffling the roofs. So cold. So cold.

III

'Did they fly in this morning then?'

'Yes, I think they got in around ten.'

'Oh. Are they both staying in Vivienne's flat?'

'Yes, of course. Gabrielle's not going for a couple of weeks.'

'That'll be difficult.'

'Yes, I suppose so.'

'Was that Vivienne on the phone earlier?'

'Yes.'

'What did she want?'

'She wants to see me.'

'When?'

'I don't know. Soon.'

'So nothing's changed? I thought, maybe, with Gabrielle being here, things might have changed.'

'No ... No, it's the same.'

'Whatever that is.'

'Whatever that is.'

'You'd better see her then, hadn't you?'

'I don't know.'

'For Chrissake, you've been wandering around, biting your nails, jumping when the phone rings. Go and see her ...'

'O.K. ... But when?'

'She has a lunch hour doesn't she?'

'Well, that's up to her, she can take one whenever she wants.'

'Well, meet for lunch.'

'I don't know.'

'I do. I can't bear to see you like this. See her. You'll have to see her sooner or later.'

'But this is awful. What will you do?'

'I'll go for a walk somewhere.'

'You don't have to go out.'

'I know. But I can't stand the thought of sitting here, knowing you're seeing her. I'll go to that bookshop, or something.'

'Do you know where it is? I could draw you a map.'

'No, it'll be O.K. I'll find it. You'd better phone her, if you want to see her today.'

'I don't know.'

'For God's sake ...'

'O.K., O.K.. Are you sure it's alright?'

'Does that matter?'

'I'll be back this afternoon.'

*

'Sorry I'm so late, I didn't think I'd be this long.'

'That's O.K.'

'What have you been doing?'

'Writing.'

'How's it going?'

'It's not.'

'Oh. What is it?'

'Are you interested?'

'Of course I'm interested. You know that.'

'Yes. I'm sorry ... How was she?'

'Not too good. Apparently it's been bad with Gabrielle.'

'Has she told her then?'

'No. No, she hasn't. She thinks it's better not to. She's just said she's changed and that it can't go on. I mean, Gabrielle's got a job in Holland. And Vivienne's working here for at least five years. So what can they do?'

'What indeed. I think it stinks, not telling her.'

'She was surprised I'd told you. She's scared you'll be angry.'

'I'm scared that I'm not.'

'Julia ... This is a bit difficult to ask, but ... since

Gabrielle doesn't know about me ... if we do see them ... could we pretend that ...'

'Pretend we're together? It is a pretence then?'

'No. No, it's not. Not entirely. I still love you, you know.'

'But not enough?'

'It's not a pretence.'

*

I watch Vivienne and Kathy sitting next to each other, exchanging cigarettes, talk and love with every look, pointing things out to each other. Forcing myself to watch them, to remember what they look like as they sit there. Both small, neat and colourful. Matching, like book-ends. I know that they look right, look self-possessed and self-possessing. Yet, somehow, an intimacy has formed between Vivienne and me. I have actually looked at her, looked in her eyes and smiled. Her eyes – dead when they look at me, like the eyes of those fish that watch her from the jars in her office. Dead, apart from the occasional moment when life sparks and fades. Can it possibly be the primitive imperative of territoriality flashing a warning? Doesn't she know I have nothing? Not even Kathy ... It's difficult to remember that; to remember not to touch her, not to laugh in certain ways, to move away from and not towards her.

*

'What's the matter? You haven't said anything all evening.'

'What do you want me to say?'

'I don't know. I can't stand it when you won't talk.'

'I don't think I can talk. I'd just scream.'

'Was it meeting Viv, this afternoon?'

'Yes. Surprisingly enough.'

'It wasn't that bad, was it?'

'Oh no. Not at all. Sitting and talking about tennis and ichthyology and fish and cartography. Fine, absolutely fine. Sitting there, looking at you two. You didn't tell me she was that attractive. I just sat there feeling huge and clumsy and stupid.'

'Don't be silly ...'

'And I could have done without her fucking

lecturing me, asking me if I played tennis and we must have a game when the weather gets better as if I'm here for a holiday or something ...'

'She was only like that because she was nervous.'

'What's she nervous about? She's got everything she wants hasn't she? It wasn't really much of a contest this afternoon, was it? I'm just getting fed up with walking through doors and finding I've lost. I'm going out to get pissed and don't come with me.'

*

Really it was no contest, although Kathy keeps telling me that it was never meant to be. How, then, did I lose? Vivienne's face, outlined against the falling snow, is perfect, is seamless. Nothing attracts like perfection: how was I to know that Kathy would come face to face with it? A picture of Kathy lying next to Vivienne in bed keeps springing into my mind.

I search the side of Kathy's face that I can see for signs of grief. All I can see is embarrassment. I am sure that if grief follows it will be mourning, not the death of a love but the death of the Kathy who would not have done this.

*

'I don't know what to do. I feel so bloody useless.'

'Why don't you go home?'

'Here was supposed to be home.'

'Go back to your friends. Please. I can't stand to see you this lonely, this lost.'

'I don't want to go home. I don't want to see what will be there for me. I wish I had someone to talk to, apart from you.'

'Talk to me then.'

'You've heard it all before. I can't go home because I'm almost paralysed by the fear of running too soon or too late.'

'God. I never thought I'd do this to you. I'm not worth all this misery.'

*

'I got a phone call today, from an old friend, from school. It was strange, I was in the shower and the phone rang and when I picked it up, there was this English voice asking for Julia.'

'Great. Why was she phoning?'

'She'd heard that I was in the States and so she phoned Vivienne, as that was the only number she had. Vivienne gave her this one.'

'What, is she living over here?'

'Yes. She's married, living in New Jersey. She's asked me to visit.'

'Great! When?'

'Can't get rid of me quickly enough?'

'I don't mean that.'

'No, I'm sorry. She's going to phone again early next week.'

*

'What are you doing? It's only half five. Why are you awake? Are you crying?'

'How can this be right when it hurts so much? How can I wake up hurting so much, if it's right?'

'What do you mean?'

'How can I leave you?'

'How can I stay?'

'Let's give it a go. Let's live together, like we planned. This can't be right.'

'Kathy ... here have a fag ... You know we can't do that. It's all worked out. I'm waiting for that call and then I'm going to stay with Halina and her husband, in New Jersey. Gabrielle's going in a couple of days, and you'll move in with Vivienne, it's all planned. I'm just waiting for a phone call. It's finished. Stop worrying. I can't worry anymore, I'm too tired. It's alright.'

'I'm not worth all this. I know it hurts. But you'll survive me, and all of this.'

'I'm fed up with surviving people. I just want to live with them.'

*

'Julia?'

'Yes.'

'Gabrielle left this morning, to fly back to Amsterdam.'

'Yes.'

'Well, when I saw Viv this morning she said maybe I ought to move to her place now. Now that Gabrielle's gone. It seems funny, after all this, for me to be staying here with you. I mean living here, still sharing the bed.'

'Yes.'

'So maybe I should go. I mean, Viv's going to New York for a week on Tuesday, so I won't see her much, unless ...'

'I see. Yes. Well, I said you'd want to go when Gabrielle did.'

'Do you think I should?'

'It's up to you.'

'It does look odd, if I don't, I mean.'

'Who's looking?'

'You don't think I should?'

'I can't tell you.'

'When's Halina calling back?'

'Sunday, maybe. Then I'll know when I can go there.'

'You can always phone me. If things get bad.'

'Yes. I've got Vivienne's number.'

'Is it O.K.? For me to go? I don't want you to be lonely.'

'I'll be alright.'

'You won't do anything stupid?'

'What do you mean?'

'You know ... anything dumb.'

'No.'

*

Kathy, I don't want you to say sorry, I don't want you to tell me to look after myself, I don't want you to tell me to keep in touch. And I don't want us to say goodbye. But over the noise of the passing trucks and cars, over the noise of a passing plane, I hear us saying it.

IV

When I woke this morning, something had changed. I lay there wondering what it was, and then I realised: through the window the sun blazed, picking out the corners and dirt in my room, lighting the moors outside. An English sun, not baking but warming.

Dressing, I watched the country respond, the moorlands opening up, Cornish granite flashing back. Downstairs, on the doormat, I found your letter, the first time I have heard from you in the months since I left. You and the sun have combined on this day to bring me to a decision of sorts. Since breakfast I have been walking, soaking up the sun, screwing my eyes up against it, listening to your letter rustling in my pocket. It is the first time I have felt warm since you left me.

When I opened your letter, over coffee and cigarettes, I don't know what I expected to find but it wasn't there. A cheque for my fare and an oblique apology has not replaced anything, has not healed or acted as a balm. But it has tuned the ears of my memory to pick out your voice from the babble of the past. Things you have said to me, since the moment of our first meeting, have been following me as I wander through the heather and scrub. For months I have been here listening to the babble, and only now has it crystallised to a voice. Years ago, in the first flush of our love you said, '*If I ever leave you, it will only be because I think you're going to leave me.*' I'd forgotten that until today. Your letter has been the tug on the one arm of the bandit and memories are pouring out, crashing into the lap of my shapeless days. Your being thousands of miles away has helped, until today.

I have built many other worlds here in these barren moors, that only I populate. I have been trying to force the hand of time, trying to hasten the moment when these past months will become: 'That time I went to the States and all those dreadful things happened.' To turn the telescope of my mind around, so that those weeks will become specks. Now that the sun's arrived I might go back home. Maybe. I might leave. It would be difficult, for I have become very used to this place, to the peace, to the scents and colours.

My memories hurt me now more than you can. I remember you saying '*No one should be anyone else's reason.*' I agree. But I didn't go thousands of miles for you to be my reason. I went to be your lover. I have many memories of those weeks in that flat, of the

140

puppet life we led as you made up your mind. Pictures of bars, clubs, restaurants, tears, smoke, water, and, of course, snow, keep flickering on and off. One image that flickers with more frequency than any other is the first I saw of you as I met you in the airport. The awful thought that I had made a mistake and that I should go home, having dismantled 'home' in order to arrive. The sun is getting hotter, a slight haze gathering around me. There's a stream near here that runs over huge slabs of granite and gravel, always cold and clear. Wading in this stream, I hear your voice once more:
'You won't do anything stupid?'
'What do you mean?'
'You know ... anything dumb.'
'No.'
And you believed me. I'd forgotten all about that, but suddenly it's helped. All these months of walking and crying and sitting in dark rooms, were, perhaps, useless, inappropriate. Because if you accepted the answer, whilst meaning the question, I really was dispensable.

I wince in the sunlight. Recollection has changed some of the things you said, or maybe I'm putting bitterness where there is none. But here in my pocket is a piece of paper on which you have written '*I hope you're looking after yourself better than I looked after you.*' It's not difficult.

Robert and Helen on the Rocks

Robert Irving stood at the kitchen window of the house he and his wife were renting on the coast of Maine, and watched the dawn of another blazing day. The house itself was a large and beautiful one, with a clapboard finish and a veranda running around three sides. The garden was carefully tended and ran down to the cliffs on which the ocean alternately sucked and pounded.

Robert Irving felt good; indeed, he felt marvellous. He and Helen had been there, alone, for three weeks now. Three weeks of sun, sea and sailing, of good food, good booze and, he thought with some surprise, good sex. Perhaps as a result of the food and liquor? he wondered as he started to prepare their breakfast. He had not been able to shake the habit of rising at six o'clock, so deeply ingrained was it for his arrival at the agency in mid-Manhattan from his New Jersey home. Still, while he was here it hardly mattered – much better to be up with the dawn and in bed by ten. Helen had asked him to wake her up so she, too, could follow this routine; left alone she would sleep until eleven. He stepped through the screen door and onto the veranda which he crossed. Walking through the garden he came to a flowering bush, the name of which he didn't know – but then, he was no gardener. He wrestled with the thick, woody stem of a flower and finally ripped it off, the stem left ragged. The heat was already rising and the humidity high, despite the breeze coming in from the sea. He felt conspicuous as he walked back to the house in a faded army shirt and battered denim shorts, holding a floppy, corpulent white flower. When he had arranged the breakfast tray he put the flower in a whiskey glass and sat the glass in pride of place, next to the syrup.

Helen Irving lay on the bed in a somnambulist reverie. The clinking and gushing of water from the kitchen below had transformed into the soundtrack of her dreams as boats went down and bells tolled in backwaters, waking her in a cold sweat. She lay on her stomach, her straw-blonde hair scratching the pillow. Her mouth was slack and her eyes, when they flickered, were shot with blood. The sheet was rucked around her feet, which kicked feebly in an attempt to move it. There was a film of sweat all over her pale body. God, she thought, barely past seven and it's like a greenhouse. The door was kicked open, jarring against a bump in the wooden flooring.

'Good morning all!' Robert cried, backing into the room and setting the tray on the bed with a flourish. Opening one bloodshot eye Helen saw a milky blob floating in front of her.

'What the hell is that?' Her voice was muffled against the pillow and she swallowed quickly to stop dribbling.

'I was hoping you'd tell me. I found a bush of them by the outhouse.' Robert smiled and pushed Helen's buttocks to and fro, rocking the bed and spilling some orange juice on the tray. 'Come on lazy, coffee's here.'

Still she lay, gathering the pieces of herself that had been scattered by sleep. Through the slits in her eyes she looked at her husband, tanned and fit in spite of the forty cigarettes he smoked each day. His grey hair was damp and combed – he had already showered. He was a handsome man, and strangely kind and gentle. She knew many people had whispered behind hands that she was far too young for him, nodding sagely as they dismissed the marriage with barely supressed snickers. But those people had not really known either of them, had not sensed the depth of companionship between them; it had been companionship that they had both needed, far more than the trappings – an appropriate word – of a conventional marriage. Helen raised herself on her elbows and smiled at him, turning her head slightly as he kissed her cheek, aware of her sour breath.

'Hello sailor,' she said with a giggle.

'Awake at last?' He lit a cigarette and motioned at the tray. 'Waffles, maple syrup, fresh-squeezed orange juice, fruit and coffee.'

'I'll be the size of a house,' she said, smiling and pleased. She was a greedy woman, always eating yet staying slim and taut.

'Ah, but you'll work it off later.' He poked her in the ribs.

'Why? What are we doing?' She turned over and put the tray on her lap.

'Well, I thought we could drive up the coast about fifteen miles and try to find a cove that's marked on the map. It's quite small but from what I can picture it would be very beautiful. We could take some food and booze and go swimming and things.'

'Sounds good,' she mumbled through a mouthful of waffle.

'There's some kind of arch or rock there which I'd like to see. I don't think the cliffs would be too steep and I think we could find some shade for you too.'

She had never understood his ability to translate maps, with their fine lines and straggles of different colours, into three-dimensional pictures of what a place would be like. He was not often wrong. She patted his thigh, leaving a smear of syrup plastering down the hairs.

'Let's do that then. We haven't been up the coast yet, have we? Only down.'

'That's why I thought it would be an idea.' Robert stood and stretched, walked to the window. 'It's a fantastic place here, isn't it? I mean, I know everyone talks about Connecticut and Massachusetts, Salem, Martha's Vineyard and everything. But it's really beautiful up here, it's really got something.' Helen reached for her cigarettes, knowing what was coming. 'I wish we could move somewhere like this, to live. It feels right, or something. I hate New York.' He stopped suddenly.

She knew what he was feeling. One night after he had drunk too much whiskey he had told her how angry and impotent he felt when he thought he wanted change. The fact was that he didn't make enough money to do what he wanted; worse was the fact that he was capable of making more if he modified his lifestyle and worked all the time that he could. But he found that he couldn't do it. He didn't want things enough to work more, work harder, compromise himself, play the political games at the agency, go to dinners and parties at which he would be bored but in the right place at the right time. He would rather spend his time with Helen, spend his money as he wished, drink and eat as well as he wanted. Sometimes he found it difficult to send the alimony cheque to Linda, his first wife, but Helen insisted that he did; she felt it was a point of honour for both of them. But she knew how he felt: a dichotomy in his character emerged when he said 'I wish ...' He wished to change as much as he wished not to and he felt this was a child-like ambivalence and evasion.

'I'll get showered, yes?' Helen jumped up from the bed and ran to the bathroom. Robert was still staring out of the window when she came out, towelling her hair, and she noticed he was edgy, although he chattered as much as ever. Knowing the sea would calm him, she hurried them both.

'What day is it?' he asked.

'Friday. Why?'

'We'll have to be back by six. I said I'd call Michael this evening.'

'Oh.' She thought of Michael, Robert and Linda's son, only a couple of years younger than her. He obviously disliked her. Arrogant and talentless he was completely different from Robert; takes after Linda she thought maliciously.

The drive along the coast diverted each of them from their own thoughts. They pointed things out to each other and stopped a couple of times to look out over the cliffs.

'They're very steep here,' Helen said, a chill running up her arms.

'They get more gentle as we go further north,' he said, peering at the hair-like markings on the map. Even that far above the foaming sea she imagined fine spray settling on her and licking her lips she tasted the tang of salt.

Finally they pulled off the road and parked on a patch of beaten earth on the seaward side. Robert slung the heavier bag over his shoulder and threw the map into the car.

'There should be a track down here. The beach itself doesn't have a name but it's not far from what I can make out.' He smiled and his enthusiasm infected her as she pulled the other bag over her shoulder. She giggled as she remembered how she'd hated summer camps when she was a child – now she was married to a man who lived his life with a permanent summer-camp mentality.

'What is it?' he asked, his smile fading.

'Nothing. Right, lead on, Captain Marvel.' She giggled again, feeling as if she were slightly drunk, knowing it was the twinge of fear that was unsettling her.

Robert went first, slithering on the loose stones and leaves strewn across the path. He turned to watch Helen slip down, clutching at branches, clumsy and graceful as a pregnant cat.

'Careful,' he shouted as she slipped and waved her arms to steady herself. He laughed as she stopped and stared at him.

'How about helping a lady?' He clambered back and took her outstretched hand and together they climbed down the wooded slope which stopped suddenly, giving way to bare craggy rocks.

'What do we do now, Captain? Jump?' Helen's face was covered with sweat as she looked at him. He tapped the rounded end of her nose saying,

'Well, if I were alone I would of course.' He squinted at the rocks ahead. 'Actually, this isn't too bad, there's enough of a ledge to go along and it seems to be dipping down to the sea.' Unconsciously they both leaned forward a little as he said this and saw the water thirty feet below. He could feel the usual delicious sense of fear and anticipation that accompanied attempting something he knew he shouldn't. It was the only time he felt really alive, yet he also knew that when Helen was with him he might want to forfeit his life to protect her.

'Lean towards the rocks with your whole body,' he told her as he stepped onto the slender ledge. 'Watch where I put my feet. If you get panicky, say something and we'll stop for a while. O.K.?'

It took them half an hour to ease themselves along the rock. Helen could feel her whole body shaking, especially her arms and hands as she clutched at small nicks in the rock, shuffling behind her husband. Both of them were pouring sweat over their clothes although they were now in the shade. He jumped the final few feet to the flat platform of rock at the bottom and held out his arms to catch her. They stood hugging each other at the foot of the cliff, plastered together with sticky sweat.

'That was horrible,' she gasped.

'But wasn't it good too?'

'I'm just not thinking about how we get back up.' He felt a ripple in his stomach as she said this, but said instead,

'You'd better put some cream on your shoulders. They look red.'

'Where is it? The cream.'

'In your bag, I think.' She rummaged in the bag, but it wasn't in there, or in his.

'I'll put the hat on, at least that will protect my face.' As she pulled the baseball cap on she had a picture of a duck going to summer camp and giggled once more. Soon she was laughing uncontrollably, the relief she felt at being on flat ground finally showing. Robert smiled faintly as he re-packed the bags. Sometimes her girl-like giggles irritated him but then he would remind himself that she was little more than a girl.

'O.K., not much further,' he said, hiking both bags onto his back. She wiped her eyes.

'Give me one, you can't carry both.'

'No, it's alright. It's just that the rocks look a bit slippery with seaweed and I think you'll be better off without yours. Step on the yellow bits, the barnacles, where you can, they'll give some grip.' Once more he walked in front of her, his canvas shoes slipping a little when he stepped on the green slime. For ten minutes or so they walked in silence, the crashing of waves and gurgling water as it slipped off the platform the only sound.

'Robert – oh, sorry, Captain Marvel?' Her voice was worried behind him.

'What?' He was intent on his walking, taken over by the rhythm of avoiding the green patches.

'Is the tide going out or coming in?'

'Eh?' He turned to her at the moment that the water spilled over and splashed against his ankles, white foam clawing up his shins. 'Oh!' He shook one foot delicately, before realising the futility of the action. Squinting at the rocks, he tried to discern a tide line, a point at which the rock-colour changed, but the waves were throwing up fountains of foam which splashed and spattered as they fell, wetting the whole platform. He looked at his watch, not knowing what else to do. 'Going out, I should think. Anyway, the beach isn't far.'

They walked on, slipping occasionally. There were boulders on the rocks that had fallen from the wooded slopes above. They had to squeeze past one enormous, almost cuboid, stone that blocked off most of the platform. Its seaward side was smooth, pounded to a fine-grained finish, yet the rest was dark and pitted, with jagged striations following the lines of its weakness. They walked further, Helen by now frankly bored with the never-changing scenery. Her legs were wet, her shoes seemed to slip more and more as the slimy green fronds forced their way into the tread. They turned a corner in the cliffs and there, indeed, was a cove.

'It's beautiful!' Helen cried, her boredom chased

away by the sight of the beach. It was a fault in the rocks, widened and deepened by a waterfall which came from the tree-filled slopes above. There were some small bushes growing where earth had been brought down by the water. There was sand, white, grey and coarse, which dipped steeply to the sea, stopping it from reaching the cliffs and ripping out the line of green. The real beauty of the place, they both knew, was that they were alone in it. Robert smiled as he savoured the fact that he had been right, that it was even more delightful than he had thought it would be. But as they were unpacking the bags and spreading out the blanket on the crunchy sand, he found a crumpled, faded cigarette packet.

There they spent the afternoon; sunbathing naked (until Helen started to pink), eating, swimming, drinking and making love, knowing that no one could see them. They behaved more like old, comfortable friends than a married couple. Even their love-making was relaxed and laughter-filled. When they swam Robert stayed near Helen, always watching her, leaving her free to flail and bob, bad swimmer that she was. She laughed at his white buttocks peeping above the choppy waves. As they walked back up the beach, dripping and flicking water from their hair, they held hands, both revelling in the adolescent feelings of their fingers touching in this old way. Finally they slept, Helen wearing Robert's long shirt, with a towel over her face, he on his front, his brown hairy arm lying heavy on her belly.

'Uh,' Robert groaned, waking suddenly as a rivulet spat on his leg. He moved creakily, feeling shortened by the hard sand and parched by the wind, salt and sun. He flexed as he stood and imagined his skin tearing like old cotton. Gulping water from a bottle he noticed that the sea had risen and was menacing the sandy shore. How long had they slept? An hour? Two? He scrabbled in his bag for his watch: half-past five. They had dozed in the sun for three hours. For the second time that day he shook his wife awake.

'Nnnng. What?'

'Time to move, it's getting late.'

'Ow!' Helen, too, moved like one in water as she pulled herself to her feet. Gingerly she fingered her legs. They stung and whitened under her touch. 'My legs are burnt.' Robert handed her the water, which she finished.

'We slept too long, that's why. We'd better leave now.'

'What time is it?'

'Five thirty. We won't be home till eight if we're not careful.'

They dressed quickly and in silence, Helen wishing she had some cream, Robert picturing the return climb. He took both bags again and set off for the bend in the cliff.

'Come on,' he called back to her.

'O.K., O.K.!' Helen shouted, hopping into her still-sodden shoes. 'Shit,' she muttered as a jagged finger nail caught her burning skin.

She joined him on a ledge, by the cliff and, like him, said nothing when she saw the sea pressing against the cliff-face, then dragging back over the platform of rock they had crossed that morning. She put her hand on his tanned shoulder.

'What now, Captain?'

'It must have been going out when I said it was.' He hadn't looked at her, only at the water. 'I didn't expect us to stay here this long ... Why didn't I think of it?' He hit the rock with a flat hand. 'Damn!'

'Because you only get confused when you think of the future, no matter how far ahead. You have a credit-card mentality,' she wanted to say. Instead she asked if there were any way they could get across. She said nothing about her legs which were beginning to tingle in the still-hot afternoon sun.

'Yes, I think there is', he said after a while. 'If you watch, it's only the third or fourth wave which really comes up a long way. The others aren't that strong and we know the platform is flat apart from those small ledges along the edge. We could run between each ledge. I think we should try it. I'll go first to check. Wait until I call you.'

For the next few minutes Helen watched him,

unaware of anything else – the roar of the water, the keening of the sea birds, a jet passing overhead – unaware of anything but Robert's silhouette as he clung to the cliff at its base, facing the rock as a wave came in, edging his way along it, moving away from her. Already he was wet to his crotch, his shorts sticking to his thighs, darker at the hem. As he had predicted, it was the fourth wave that was the wildest. Now it came racing over the platform, hit the wall at his feet and rose to his chest as he sought a hand-hold. The spume hit his face and neck, he was lifted for a moment, the bags floating by his shoulders. Then he found a groove and held tightly as the water sluiced away between his legs. Glancing at the momentarily exposed platform he ran to a ledge and stood panting and shaking.

'Are you alright?' Helen's voice sounded faint and strained. He held up his hand, waiting for the adrenalin shot to pass.

'Yes,' he shouted finally. 'Are you ready?'

Helen looked at the divide between them: it was like the earth rocking back and forth, a lottery of good timing. Her burns forgotten, she waited for the call.

'Now!' he shouted.

She jumped from her safe perch and nearly fell.

'Stick as close to the rocks as you can!'

She hugged her body to the warm, scratchy surface, her hands searching for grooves, quick and fluttery as birds. Her knees were scraped. All she could hear was her own rasping breath.

'Hurry!'

The water sucked at her knees. She felt rather than heard the fourth wave as it hit the edge of the platform. She broke away from the rockface and ran towards the voice she could hear. As the wave hit her she fell sideways. A hand grabbed her flailing arm and held her as she lay in the water, pulled first one way and then the other. Gasping for air, swallowing the brackish water, she lost her sense of time and space. She felt as if she were tumbling over and over, she tried to breathe but her mouth was full. Suddenly it was gone; she could feel the barnacles grazing her stomach. A voice, now, saying,

'Up. Come on, up here before the next one.' She was hauled up by her arm, pulling at the socket. Then Robert was behind her, bending her over and pushing at her stomach. She heaved water from her guts, which splattered on the ledge and was washed away by the water swilling over it. Eventually she stopped, her throat raw, her eyes stinging.

'That was rather a close one,' she said weakly, still doubled over. Robert sighed softly, sensing she had recovered, that she still worked.

Twice more they made dashes from one paltry ledge to another, avoiding the fourth wave. By now they were both wet and tired, both shaking with fear and adrenalin. Both bled from grazes on hands, elbows and knees; the blood was diluted by water, staining their bodies with delicate pink-laced fans.

'I don't think I can do it again.' Helen looked at her husband, her face reddened by the sun and exertion. 'I'm too tired. I just can't keep it up.'

If only I were alone, he thought, I might be able to make it. His chest hurt as he looked at her cuts and burning skin.

'There's only one thing I can think of – that rock that we passed, the big square one, it's just around the corner, really not very far, maybe ten yards ...'

'Yes?'

'We could climb on that and wait for the tide to turn, to go out.'

'What time is it now?'

'Watch out!' A wave smashed over the platform and burned towards them, bubbling with anticipation. Robert threw one arm around Helen and braced them against the cliff. Water filled the air around them, they floated, then dropped, Robert's legs rigid against the ledge. The wave fell back, disappointed.

'Christ al-fucking-mighty!' Helen shouted, pushing his arm away, and now he saw that she was furious. The last onslaught had left her with a cut on her forehead, making her seem even more violent. 'Let's get to this frigging rock, I'm not staying here.' She even gave him a small shove, sending him off the ledge.

'O.K., same again!' he shouted as he sprinted towards the rock.

The rock was wet only on one side, near the water. There would be enough room and some safety. They opened the bags to find that everything was wet, even the cigarettes. Slowly, without speaking, they spread the blanket and then scattered everything else around them, hoping it would dry in the weakening sun. Helen covered her legs with a damp towel as Robert sat, aching for a cigarette, with water spraying him arrhythmically.

So they sat, naked, surrounded by the debris of their idyllic afternoon, nicked and scratched, sore and aching, tired and resentful, bathed in a pale light.

'As I asked, before we were so rudely interrupted, what time is it?' Her voice had a rasping quality, like the barnacle-littered rocks below.

'Quarter of seven.'

'How long will it take to go out?'

'I'm not sure. A couple of hours maybe.'

'What time will it be then, Captain?'

'Eh? Nine or so.'

'And it will be dark.' Robert looked at her when she said this, only to see her profile – she had not looked at him since they had clambered up to their resting point. He picked up two cigarettes and saw they were mottled with brown stains, but quite dry.

'Cigarette?' He held one out to her and lit it with the cheap plastic lighter which had survived unscathed.

'We can't get up that tiny ledge in the dark.' Smoke billowed in front of Helen's face as she said this.

'I know that,' he snapped.

'So what do we do?'

'It might help if you shut up and let me think.'

Helen turned her back to him and smoked, savouring the nicotine. She felt that she didn't really care much any more. Robert stared out to the dull horizon, knowing exactly what they would have to do, knowing that she knew too and knowing that she would make him say it. He threw the yellow butt into the water and watched it bob.

'Since we can't get up the cliff again in the dark, I think we'll have to stay here for the night.' There, it had been said.

'How long?'

'Till dawn, maybe, till it's light.'

'When's that?'

'About six.'

'We're going to be here until six tomorrow morning?'

'Well, at least the tide will be out then too.'

Helen turned at last to look at him.

'Robert, why didn't you think of this?'

'I don't know.' He didn't.

'Let me tell you why, Robert. Give me another cigarette.' He knew how few there were left but gave her a lit one. 'The reason you didn't think of it is because you never think of anything, never think anything through to the end. Your life is full of beginnings, there just aren't any endings. Unless, of course, you count your divorce from Linda, which is an ending of sorts. But I doubt that you planned that as such. Maybe you did, I don't know.'

'God, I said I'd call Michael tonight. He'll be worried.'

'Hang on, I'll get a dime and you can call him from the nearest payphone.'

'Shut it, will you? What's the point of going on? I'm sorry, I should have thought, should have checked. Going on won't help. We're stuck here and that's that.'

'All very well for you, buddy, but I've got sharp rocks sticking up my ass, cuts all over me and my skin is blistering.'

'If you sit where I am you get wet. Take your pick.'

Helen rolled over, tucked into a ball and cried. As she lay there she felt the viscous, still-warm fluid oozing out between her legs, a legacy of the afternoon as much as the sodden blanket and damp tobacco. Anger rose up in her once again; more than anything she wanted to wash herself clean, wash away the remains of this man who she could never entirely trust but who had captured her with his gentleness. She looked over the rock's edge, seeing only bubbling foam. At that moment the sun slipped, touching the sea. A breeze blew in and Helen's burnt skin puckered, the small blonde hairs that covered her body became prickly and taut. She began to shiver uncontrollably as she lay on her side, the sharp nodes and ridges of the rock digging into her small body. Now the rock itself felt warm, was giving out the heat that it had hoarded during the day, she wanted to sprawl on it but it hurt too much.

'You've never told me anything like that before. About endings.' Robert's voice startled her.

'No, well, I doubt that it's struck me quite so forcibly before.'

'It's a thing that you often do – when something gets to you you just think about it and get angry, but you don't say anything until months later, and then you recall where we were, what day it was, what was said – everything. So I assume that you must keep thinking of it, to keep it fresh in your memory. Why don't you just say it when you feel it? Instead of building up a load of angst which isn't in proportion to what happened?'

'I'm cold.'

'The clothes are still damp, don't put them on.'

'I know that.'

'Come here, body heat's best.'

'No.'

Robert stared at his wife's back, shaking on the blanket. She had curled so tight that he could see each of her vertebrae pushing against her pale shiny skin. God, but she could be childish. He wanted to shake her, to grab her arms and shake her. As the moment passed the sun dropped below the water.

'We're stuck here and all you can think about is Michael.'

'What?'

'The first thing you thought of was Michael. You don't really give a damn about me.' Robert had to strain to hear this last over the sound of the water.

'Michael is my son,' he said icily.

'Michael is a shit.'

'There — typical example of what I was saying. You just let things build up ...'

'If you had no idea of how I felt then it shows you're not exactly sensitive to my feelings. I'm thirsty.'

'What?'

'I'm thirsty.' He handed her the half-empty bottle of wine they had started with their lunch — was it only that long ago? Helen sat up to drink, her shaking hands making it difficult. 'I'd love some coffee,' she said, handing him the bottle. Robert smiled and said he would too. He felt himself trying to defuse the situation, to smooth it over. As usual it was he who had to draw the sting from this scorpion's tail. But then, Robert knew the power of words — he had sat in hot, summer houses with Linda and felt the cold winds blowing through them.

'Look, I don't want to argue.'

'Who's arguing?' Helen asked pointedly.

They sat in silence, both wondering what had soured them. Love would have warmed them, made them feel drier, but instead there were only barbed words and two naked, shivering backs turned to each other. Not for the first time Robert thought how fragile even this relationship was, how it crumbled and fell into dark corners with a careless touch. He wondered how much anyone had to care before it ceased to happen.

'Oh my God!' Helen suddenly sat up and turned to him, her left hand held out, the bloodied fingers stretched apart.

'What? What is it?' He snatched her hand and twisted it over, looking for a wound.

'It's gone — my ring, it's gone!' Then he saw the thin white line where her wedding ring had been, a pale, embarrassed imitation. Instinctively he looked around, hoping to catch its glint on the rock's surface. But it had been a young ring, barely a year old, Helen's finger had not had a chance to grow thick around it, to grow so fleshy that the ring could only be worked off with soap. As she had followed Robert on his dashes, her ring had been torn from her, loosened by the cold. Something gun-metal and sharp swam through Robert's guts. He moved to his wife and hugged her close, stroking her matted, damp hair as she rocked back and forth sobbing.

So they faced the endless night together, now clinging on to each other, each unwilling to let the other go. The blanket dried as the water eventually gurgled away; the heat of the rock ebbed slowly, eking out its warmth. Both considered for a moment the fact that it had been a loss which had brought down the wall of words they had been erecting between themselves. Robert promised Helen another ring, exactly like the last and then held her as she slept fitfully, mumbling and squeaking like a kitten. He, too, dozed for a while, until the water advanced again and spattered them. They spent the early hours sharing cigarettes and the last of the wine, waiting for the brush of light on the skyline. When it finally appeared, they were not satisfied, willing the sun to move more quickly, to throw more heat. When the cold, dead light of dawn was with them they looked around, disappointed, both expecting to see a battlefield, littered with broken staves and horses, mangled rocks and the smashed keels of boats.

Helen's head was spinning – a carnival of her childhood fears had played themselves out as she slept. Nearly always Robert had taken most of her away from them and it was for that she loved him. She looked at him as her head cleared.

'Can we go now please?' Her voice was cracked and pitted, her throat dry.

'I think I've had enough too,' he squeaked back.

They pulled on the dry, stiff clothes, Helen breaking blisters on her shoulders, uncaring. Tentatively they allowed themselves to think but not yet speak of coffee, orange juice and hot soapy water. Robert motioned down to the platform, now exposed and glittering once more. They climbed off the rock and hobbled towards the ledge trailing up to the trees. She did not protest when he took her bag before beginning the inching climb. It was easier going up the cliff, despite their stiffening limbs and the scabs that were broken off by the rocks or opened by flexed skin. Neither said a word as they struggled up the dusty slope, Robert hauling his wife up the steepest part which gave out on the patch where their car was parked. Helen smiled when she saw it, cracking her lips.

The drive was as silent as the walk, the heat mounting. Robert drove fast, imagining waterfalls of juice, his throat constricting as he tried to swallow. Helen dozed, her head lolling on the window, dreaming of bowls of cornflakes, soaked in ice-cold milk. They stumbled up the drive to the house and pushed open the kitchen door. Robert held up his hand, telling her to slow down as she walked to the fridge. He poured each of them a small glass of water which they later agreed had tasted better than any fifteen-year-old whiskey. He whisked an egg and honey into some milk and added some sugar, a drink which plastered down the barbs in their throats and cured their muteness.

'Shit, that was good,' Helen croaked, wiping the white moustache away with the back of her hand. He was relieved by her tone, knowing that what danger there had been had passed. In the silence of the walk and drive he had not been able to gauge the depth of her resentment, had not been able to dip a conversational finger into the waters of her discontent to feel the temperature. He sighed softly and smiled, wincing as his face cracked.

'Do you want to have a bath now and eat later? Or the other way around? As he spoke Robert opened his arms and Helen came to him.

'Bath, then eat. Lots,' she muttered into his shoulder.

In the bathroom they stripped off their clothes and ran a deep bath. Helen added oil and a scented bubblebath, insisting that Robert share it. They washed each other gently and lathered each other's hair. After they had dried themselves off Robert dressed the worst of their cuts and grazes; he was startled as she held out her hand to see the ring's absence for he had forgotten its loss.

'Later, after we've slept, we'll go into town and buy another.'

'It doesn't have to be today.'

'Yes, yes it does.' He didn't want to say that it scared him – her not wearing his ring – but she sensed it and nodded, mussing his greying hair.

'O.K. Captain.'

'I think I've been demoted.'

'Never. Let's eat.'

'Wait, I'll put some camomile on you.' When he had finished he laughed, the first time in a long time, or so it seemed. She was like a mummy, almost completely white.

'So laugh, I can still eat.'

And so she did. He marvelled at her as she ate bacon, eggs, hash browns, mushrooms and tomatoes, demanded waffles and syrup and ate these. To finish: toast, marmalade and some cold pasta she found in the fridge. He had little, feeling too tired.

They both groaned as they lowered themselves slowly onto the bed, pulling up only the crisp white sheet. He wanted very much to make love to her. Instead he laid his hand on her stomach and could feel the lump that was her breakfast. Lying next to each other, staring at the blank ceiling, they savoured the thought of sleep but pushed it away a little longer.

'Robert?'

'Hmmm?'

'What I said about endings?'

'Hmmm?'

'It doesn't really matter.'

'I think it does. I know what you mean and it's a failing. Or rather, just for me it works fine, but not now.'

'Most times I like living on an open-ended ticket. Yesterday was just bad luck. Or is it today?' Her voice was slurred and her head tilted towards him.

'Hey.' He nudged her gently. 'Hey.'

'What?'

'Would you like to live here? Around here, I mean?'

'Yeah.'

'Then we shall. I'm going to do it. We can be here by Christmas.'

'Wonderful – potatoes and fish baked on an open fire.' With this thought she fell asleep.

Robert Irving felt good; indeed, he felt marvellous. He watched his wife sleep as he planned his moves. He had come to see the fragility of his life in a different way. They were not Captain Marvel and Batgirl but they were something. He vowed to keep them always warm, so that the cold winds would not be noticed. With that thought he, too, fell asleep, oblivious to the ringing of the phone as Michael again tried to reach him.

Less of the Spaghetti Legs

'Hello? Jo?'
  'Yes.'
  'It's Lindsay.'
  'Yes. How's it going?'
  'It's bad, very bad. Much worse than we thought it would be.'
  'I gather you've told him.'
  'Yes, a few hours ago.'
  'Well, what's wrong? I mean, what's happening?'
  'Nothing. That's it: absolutely bloody nothing.'
  'Nothing? What, he hasn't reacted?'
  'Oh yes, he's reacted – he laughed and then shouted a lot for a while. He's not accepting it. You know, like one of those *decree nisi* things or something that you have to actually hold in your hand before it's considered served. He just won't open his hand to take it. He won't even talk about it. He's just sitting in the front room listening to music, reading the paper, as though nothing's happened. What do you do when someone behaves like that? What *can* I do? I've told him and that's that.'
  'He wasn't even angry?'
  'Well, the only thing he seemed angry about was that he trusted you and liked you and he thought you'd let him down in some way.'
  'I let him down? What on earth do you mean?'

'Don't ask me, that's what he said. I've just been sitting out here in the kitchen wondering what to do next. I don't see what I can do. I mean, do I pack my bags and come over to your place, or what?'

'I don't think you can do that, we agreed it wasn't on. You have to explain to him what's happened, it's unfair not to.'

'Right now I feel as though my leaving like that might be the only way of provoking some kind of reaction. I think it's crazy that he hasn't done anything – I thought he'd smash the place up, or something.'

'What was he laughing about?'

'Eh?'

'You said that he laughed when you told him, what was he laughing about?'

'He said that he'd been expecting something far worse when I started to tell him. He laughed because he was relieved. Don't you see? He doesn't think that this counts.'

'Doesn't count? What, because I'm a woman, it doesn't count?'

'Yes, that's it exactly. Now, if you were a man, the situation would be serious and he'd be tearing the place down.'

Jo turns away from the wall and stares out of the window at the indifferent sky. All day she has stayed by the phone, waiting for this call, waiting to be told what has happened. From the moment of waking she has hung from the meat-hook of a not-yet-made decision. The small table by the phone is covered with playing cards, some stacked in piles, some scattered in twos and threes. There is no order in the game: the game she plays by herself, a game born many years before in lonely, sulky sitting rooms overlooking oceans and beaches. She knows when she bends rules and when she breaks them, although she could not explain to anyone, least of all to herself. She lights a cigarette and inhales deeply, imagining the smoke rolling, rolling into every rounded air-bag in her chest. What to say next? This, of all things, this nothingness, she has not expected. As the phone rang she sighed and leaned back, away from the noise, thinking 'Now I will know. Now something will begin or end.' But instead there is this laugh, laughed hours before, and there is this rustling of paper and a blank, solid back presented to her, like a smooth, shaven face. She must now hurt to get what she wants, when, like everyone, she would rather have been given it.

'Jo, you still there?'

'Uh? Yes, I'm here.'

'Well, what should we do?'

'I don't know, I just can't think. Tell me exactly what you told him, and how. Is it O.K.? To talk, I mean. Can he hear you?'

'Yes, it's fine. Like I said, he's listening to music and having a drink as though nothing's happened. He can't even hear me.'

'Go on then.'

'I knew I had to tell him today, otherwise I'd never get the nerve up. So I suggested that we went for a drink at lunchtime, since I thought it would be better if there were others around, then he wouldn't be able to make a scene. You know what he's like, he flies off the handle about anything. Anyway, I didn't tell him straightaway, we just sat and talked about things. I can't remember a word of that because all I could think of was what I had to say. Then suddenly I knew the moment had arrived, even though he was talking. I just butted in and said, "Simon I've got something to tell you that will hurt you, and I'm sorry that it will." Then I told him.'

'What did you actually say? It's important.'

'Um ... something like: "Jo and I have been lovers for a long time now and our relationship has reached the point where I can't lead a double life any longer. I've thought about it a lot, and I'm leaving you to live with Jo. I'm sorry it happened like this, but I have to tell you." Something like that.'

'And he laughed?'

'No, not at first. He looked furious and didn't say anything for a long time. Then he said, "Joe? Joe Tylberg?" and I said, "No, Jo Radcliffe." Then he laughed and said, "You had me worried for a while."'

'Oh shit.'

'You see what I mean?'

'Did you talk to him any more about it?'

'Of course I bloody did. All he was interested in was where and when. And eventually, how.'

'Oh Christ. I don't know why I'm so surprised, but I am. Um ... I don't know what to suggest.'

'You have to suggest something. If I can't come over to your place, then I'll have to do something else, but I don't know what.'

'Look Lindsay, it's up to you, not me. I can't advise you about what you should do. You know that, you know why.'

'No, I don't know why. At the moment I feel in need of some support and you're not giving me any. You're just washing your hands of the whole business.'

'I'm not. It's just that since you're the one who's giving up something and not me, then I think that you should make all the decisions.'

'You sound as though you don't give a damn.'

'Oh God.'

She doesn't understand what I'm trying to say. How can I tell her what to do? Already Jo's mind has raced forward, to a point not yet reached, which may never be reached: the argument she will have with Lindsay on a numberless, dry day, standing face to face, shouting across the schism of someone's making. The day when Lindsay will say: I left Simon for you, you told me to leave him, you encouraged me, how could I have listened to you? These words echo in Jo's mind as she stands listening to her lover's breathing whistling down the lines. How much easier to say 'Come, come here and everything will be alright.' Easy now, easy now. But what of that day hovering in the future? Easier then?

'Lindsay, it really is up to you. But I think you should make sure that he understands.'

'How?' A pause as Lindsay tries to breathe, in, out, and to smother the quaver that has bent her voice. 'Sorry. How? Do I just keep talking to him? When he's not even bloody listening?'

'Well, yes. What else is there to do? I can't think.'

'It's alright for you, sitting at home, waiting for me

to get through this. What do you think it's like for me?'

Alright? To have sat here watching the shadows change and the smoke floating through the room, waiting for this call. And now having to start the vigil all over again. More time without change, seemingly timeless.

'Look, try to talk to him or something, and call me later.'

'Thanks a lot. You've been a great help.'

The streets around Jo's flat are bustling, noisy, the day coming to an end with a clunk of plastic on plastic as she cradles the phone on its rest. The sky darkens and lights flick on, reflected from the tarry, obsidian-like roads, making everything seem much busier than it is. Jo can hear the swish of buses and the cries of children chasing each other as she stands by her window, looking. She is trying to perceive things as they are, to put herself in relation to them. Perspective, distances and light all play on her and with her as she stands, looking. She is here, in this flat, in the midst of all this bustle, a part of this life that swirls around her. But she feels caged, isolated. Like a milky suspension hanging in clear liquid. She can't do it, she can't fit herself in anywhere. The telephone squats by the small table: smug-pug. She longs to run out, to thump down the stairs and out onto the streets, to walk and lose herself amongst all those people. But she knows she can't, she must wait for another summons, another call ringing through this ever-darkening room, telling her to answer Lindsay once more, still not knowing what to say.

She is increasingly unsure of herself and of all the things around her. To have an idea is so different from having no idea. How has this happened? Suddenly she feels panic, feels that she is losing her mind. She realises that she is breathing too quickly, but in slowing her breathing she starts to think about it and finds herself forcing her lungs to become bellows, drawing in the stale, pregnant air and then forcing it out, pushing with her throat. Look out of the window:

everything is as it should be, everything is fine. The panic returns; for if she becomes too slow, she may stop altogether. Somewhere in-between, try for somewhere in-between. Walk around the room, light a cigarette, keep moving, but stay calm.

She may not phone for hours, perhaps not until tomorrow. No, if she doesn't phone until tomorrow, I'll die, I know I will. If she doesn't call soon I'll have to phone her, I can't bear the waiting. But then, what do I say? I am still at a loss for words, for ideas, all I have left are my feelings, and I trust those less and less. I know that I love Lindsay. That I know; that will keep my legs moving. But what if she doesn't phone back? What if Simon becomes the little boy that he is, in order to keep her? So much easier to walk away from a man than a child. I wonder if he knows that? Of course he does, we all do. Does he have it in him to be dignified, to acknowledge defeat and change and make it easy for us, for Lindsay? He has said that he loves her, has been saying it for years, but only now will the quality of that love become evident. For if he changes in order to keep her then he demeans all that has gone before. But if he lets this slip through his fingers by loving her enough to let her go where she wants he will always wonder if he should have fought for what he wants.

Jo is starting to lose herself once more as she realises that by doing nothing, by saying nothing, she may lose Lindsay. Should she call back to say 'I want you, don't think that I don't', or 'I was wrong, come over here now, it's best'? Yet, if Lindsay decides not to come but to stay with Simon, then that's what she wants, more than an unknown life with Jo, which means that life would not have worked anyway. Lindsay must decide. The room around Jo, as she walks in circles and then paces between one wall and another, seems to close in on her with each of her turns, but still she cannot leave it, still the phone has not rung.

Play the cards, start another game. Jo forces herself to sit down, becoming conscious of her breathing again as she lights a cigarette. In, out, in, out. Gather the cards into a neat-edged pile. Shuffle them, creating chaos out of order. Play the cards, play the cards. Deal with probabilities. For that is how Jo plays, mistrusting intuition. Jerkily she deals herself her own cards, desperate to lose herself. But no matter how she tries to become the young girl she was when she made up this game, to become that innocent, she fails. She sits back and, as she does so, throws up the cards she holds in her hand, up into the air above the blank face of a Queen. The cards flip through the bands of light and darkness that flicker and seem to move as the numbers and colours flick on and off in a sequence that is without meaning. As they fall and land with clicks and clacks on the table, smothering that blank face, some slither to the floor, taking others with them. Finally, all that is left of the game is the ace of diamonds, winking at Jo through the half-cover of the other cards.

The phone rings as Jo snorts in self-disgust. A calm descends on the room. At least she has not been cheated of this moment. Perhaps that is what she was worried about?

'Jo?'

'Yeah.'

'Hello. Sorry I've taken so long to phone back.'

'That's alright. How're things?'

'A bit better in some ways, worse in others. I did what you said and went and talked to him about it. He's finally realised that I mean it, and that it's serious because of that. I sort of started to pack and I think that's when it hit him.'

'So, what's happened?'

'Oh God, it's awful in a way. You know that I thought he'd get violent? Well, quite the opposite. He's been crying and crying and won't stop. I suppose I thought he'd pretend not to care.'

'Would that have been better?'

'What do you mean?'

'Well, if he'd done that, pretended not to care, you'd either have been offended or you would have wondered if he were crying once you left.'

'What's the point of saying that?'

'None, I suppose. What happens now?'

'Um ... This is a bit difficult to ask. He really is upset and sort of ... scared.'

'Yes?'

'He wants to see you.'

'Me?'

'Yes. He's been asking me to call you and ask you to come over for ages. I've been trying to tell him it's not such a good idea. I mean, at first I thought it was because he wanted to beat you up or something. But it's not, really it's not. I think he genuinely wants to see you, as someone that he gets along with.'

Jo rocks back and forth in the chair, sees the red and white pointed card still leering at her. She presses the heels of her hands into her eyes until she sees the eclipse of the sun.

'Do you think I should come over?'

'I'm not sure. I think you should, because you two do get along, and maybe you can say something to him to make him feel better. But then, maybe I just want to see you, for you to be here. It would make things so much better for me. I feel as though I haven't seen you for ages.'

'Yes, that's how I feel too.'

'What can I say, to him?'

'I don't know, but in a way I feel that this is wrong, what we've been doing, that you're not here. Especially when we all know each other.'

'You *do* know why I didn't come in the first place? What we said about it being your loss and not mine? That I ought not to get involved because I'd try to get you anyway, no matter what was happening?'

'Yes, of course I remember all that. We bloody talked about it enough. Somehow, now that it's all happening, it's different. It seems silly for you to be there and not to be involved because it's about all three of us.'

'I suppose so.'

'So?'

'So what?'

'Are you going to come?'

'I have to don't I?'

'No, not if you don't want to.'

'Whether I want to or not, I have to come.'
'How long will you be?'
'I'll drive over, I suppose. Um ... half an hour.'
'I'll see you then.'
'Yes.'
Both women stand staring at nothing in their separate rooms, miles apart, waiting. Neither can finish this, to start the next bout of madness.
'Lindsay?'
'Mmmm?'
'I love you.'
'I love you too.' Lindsay slams the phone down and runs away from it.

Jo moves around her flat, tidying things away, finding a jacket, stacking plates. She feels she is living on borrowed time. Time borrowed from when? Other, happier times? Making those times themselves shorter by hours and days. Routine is the only way that Jo can see out of this maze of emotion. Doing ordinary things, as though nothing were happening. Checking the gas is off, the doors are closed, one light left on, car keys and money in pocket. As she leaves, locking and checking the front door, she wonders in what way she will have changed when she stands in that room once more. What will have happened? Suddenly she wants to know the ending of the unexpected story; to be the listener, urging the speaker on to the end: 'Who does Lindsay end up with? Who gets hurt? Tell me. Tell me.' Instead, she must live through what will follow. And indeed, she can change the ending, it has not yet been written. The awareness of the chain of moments that stretch out behind and in front of her, the necessity of succession, does not leave her as she walks to her car: the future is a tightrope. Opening the car door she savours the thought that she can do nothing but drive for the next half hour. That the following thirty minutes are spoken for.

But as she weaves a tortuous route through London, worked out months before by Lindsay (who had giggled endlessly as she gave one direction after another that led them down one-way streets, to dead ends and to cul-de-sacs) she finds that she must think of what is to come, what she will have to face when she arrives at Lindsay's flat. Why is Simon doing this? She has a double image of him and she cannot force the two pictures to gel into one: the Simon she knows and the Simon she will see soon. His face swims into her already dislocated mind, wearing an expression of indifference, smudged with satisfaction: this is the Simon she knows. Does she get on with him, as he is now claiming? Perhaps he thinks so, but he is just a table-padder, a room-filler to her. She had asked him questions about his life and he had answered, content with knowing nothing about hers; perhaps that is what makes him think that there is some bond between the two of them. And, of course, he had never sensed anything sexual about her but had treated her as he would an old school friend. Why, then, is he doing this? Why does he want her to watch this collapse? He has become a small boy as she had guessed that he would. He is saying to Lindsay, 'See, without you, I collapse. I am nothing' and she may believe him. Is he going to stand both women in front of him to watch this performance, accusing them with his tears? Implying, by his submissiveness, that women, mothers, daughters, wives, lovers, all give too little of themselves. And, if they seem still not to believe him, he will point to his child-like state and accuse Lindsay of leaving him even then. She can walk away from anything, uncaring. Uncaring. A flash of rage zips through Jo as she sits in her car at traffic lights, listening to the noise all around her.

Men, in their cars, honking, shouting, waving their arms. Stepping out in front of her to cross the road, looking at her as if she is not even there. Men strutting in and out of shops, hands in pockets, staring about them. Men spilling in and out of pubs. Men standing with their feet splayed, arms crossed over their bellies, rocking on their heels. Men's bellies; curving softly out over the belts of their trousers, sagging. Men pushing their bellies before them, as women push their prams, equally proud. Men turning to watch a girl walk past and then turning back to talk, bellies almost touching.

What is happening to me? I've never felt like this before – felt this deep, flowing hatred towards people I don't even know. Panic rolls over Jo's legs and she feels them settle in a pool of concrete around the pedals at her feet. The traffic wheeling around the roundabout spins in front of her, stopping her getaway from this point of fear. Suddenly a grinding jolt throws her forward, ramming her against the nylon of her seat belt. Her head snaps back and then rolls lazily. All she can think, as her car sits slewed across the dotted line, jutting into the ferris wheel of other cars, is that the ash of her cigarette has broken off and is burning the carpet under the seat.

A deadly deliberation descends as she unbuckles the belt and feels with her finger tips for the glowing tobacco and, finding it, throws it out of the window. Cars still pass her, the passengers craning to stare as she draws breath. Stepping out of the car she rolls her head once more and a stabbing pain sears through her temples. But as she rubs them the pain recedes slightly leaving a dull pounding. Jo walks to the car that is nestling into the buckled wing of her own and knocks on the driver's window with her red, bony knuckles. It is only then that she realises her hand is bleeding; she must have smashed it into the steering wheel as she was flying forward.

The two young men in the damaged car continue to talk excitedly behind the protection of their glass, glancing at Jo as they gesticulate. Jo raps on the glass again and rolls her hand in the air, telling them to open the bloody window. The frightened faces in front of her suddenly turn to look behind them, and spin around. The driver reaches for the keys to turn on the engine and Jo realises what they are about to do. She grabs the door handle and pulls at it but, as she had guessed, it is locked. She whips her hand away as the car shoots back, ripping down the side of her Mini, which still thrusts into a stream of traffic. Paint peels and flakes, metal bends as Jo jumps back from the noise and violence of what these men are doing. She kicks ineffectually at the driver's door as he spins away, with a smell of burning rubber as a tyre grates along the damaged wing. Jo watches, standing in the middle of the road, as they swing out into the roundabout, grazing a post, and away. Running back to her car she mutters the registration to herself and once in the car scrabbles for a pen and cigarette packet to write it down. Her hands shake so much she can barely make out what she is writing.

'Bastards. Bastards. Bastards. Fucking bastards.'

Slamming her door she turns the ignition and screams away, hardly watching where she is going. For minutes she drives as though hers is the only car on the road; swerving between lanes, shooting lights, weaving into small spaces, until a cyclist wobbling in front of her forces her to thump on her brakes. Then she sits, panting and swearing, and waits for the lights to change, pulling away slowly as the green light winks on. Looking at her hand she sees the blood is now dark, sickly maroon, flaking away as she rubs it with spit-dampened fingers. Smearing it over her wrist. As she makes a fist, tiny ears of skin, bunched over her fingers, flap back to reveal diamonds of raw, oozing flesh. It begins to smart as Jo becomes herself. She realises she is still driving to Lindsay's flat and, thinking about it, knows it is the only thing she can do. Gradually the banging of her head and heart fade as she gets to the end of her journey. Parking, the pain in her neck returns as she swivels to look over her shoulder. The engine murmurs to silence and Jo stares at the squares of light that are the windows of the flat she knows so well. Behind those squares are two people waiting for her, perhaps more scenes of violence and noise. Climbing out of the Mini she winces and decides not to look at the damage. (So much damage being done.) As she crosses the road, the flat door opens and the silhouette of Lindsay watches her.

'Hello. You've been a long time. Thank God you're here, he's not any better.'

The women stand awkwardly in the hallway, angled away from each other, aware as they have never been before of the man in the other room. They do not touch as they would have done otherwise but shift slightly, increasing the distance between them.

'I have to go to the bathroom. I won't be a minute.'

The rose-pink water swirls away, stained with the blood Jo is washing off her hand. She sees that it is bruised rather than cut, with only one patch of skin hanging by a line on one finger. She pulls this off and wraps the finger in a plaster. Rinsing her face in cold water, she presses her eyelids shut, squeezing them, hoping that when she opens them everything will be alright. Groping for a towel she bangs her bruised hand against the towel rail.

'Shit.'

'Are you O.K.?' Lindsay is standing outside the door, waiting to be escorted into Simon's presence. Or is it the other way round?

'Yes, I'm fine,' says Jo, opening the door and switching off the light.

'Do you want to see him?'

'Now I'm here, I may as well.'

'Come on then.'

Walking down the hall Jo flicks a look into the bedroom and sees cases yawning open and clothes in heaps on the floor. She feels very tired, wants to sprawl on that bed, wrapped in Lindsay's clothes and sleep and sleep. Instead, she follows Lindsay's back down the passage to the closed door behind which is Simon.

'Jo's here, Simon. Simon?' Lindsay looks around the door and motions Jo into the room. In the corner, on an old two-seat sofa, sits Simon, elbows on knees, hands dangling between his legs. Jo coughs and shuffles into the room.

'Hello Simon.'

He looks up slowly and seems to have to scan the small room to find Jo. Seeing her he blinks and lowers his head again, a fresh spasm of tears shaking his body, sunk in the sofa.

'Do you want a drink?' Lindsay has moved away to the door and is looking at Jo.

'Yes, yes, that would be nice.'

'What? Tea, coffee, scotch, gin?'

'Scotch please. A small one.'

'O.K.' She turns and is gone.

What do I do now? Ask him what the matter is? This is mad. Jo has never felt so alone, has never wished more for some third person to be there. She glances at the doorway again, hoping to see her lover. Simon sputters to a halt and the room falls silent. He stares at Jo through bleary eyes, swallowing time and time again. He tries to talk, but his throat is too tight and his head jerks to one side. Coughing, he tries again.

'I trusted you, do you know that?'

Jo takes off her jacket and lays it over the back of a chair. Lighting a cigarette she sits opposite the child at the other end of the room.

'Yes, I know that. But I'm not sure what you mean by trust.'

'Don't start all that crap. You know what I bloody mean.'

'All I'm trying to say is that you're making it sound as though it was only your trust for me that was keeping you and Lindsay together. And that's stupid, it's just not true.'

'Don't play silly games with words, I trusted you.'

'Does that mean you didn't trust Lindsay?'

This starts him crying again. Lindsay comes in with two tumblers of scotch, for Jo and herself. She is dry-eyed as she sits in a third corner and watches Simon. She sips her drink and then turns to Jo and waggles two fingers in the air, asking for a cigarette. Jo throws the pack to her, reminding herself that she must not forget it – it has the registration number on it.

'What are you going to do now?' Simon has changed since Lindsay came in and is sitting up, talking aggressively.

'Right now?' Smoke billows in front of Lindsay as she asks.

'Yes, right now. Are you going to take her away?' he asks Jo.

'Don't talk about me like that, I'm not a dog.' Lindsay speaks quite distinctly, with no trace of emotion. She's got none left, thinks Jo. I've been asked over here to take over where she's left off.

'Simon, I haven't come to take Lindsay away. I've come because Lindsay said you wanted to see me.'

'Yes, I do. I just want to ask if you realise that what she's doing to me she'll do to you sooner or later?' He smiles a crooked, frightening smile. Lindsay sighs violently and rolls her eyes, shaking her head.

'I hope not.'

'Of course you bloody hope not. How long have you two been doing this? She won't tell me.'

'What difference does that make?'

'Tell me.'

'No. Why do you want to know?'

'I've got the bloody right to know, haven't I?' He leaps up suddenly and Jo flinches, the pain in her neck whipping through her head. Grabbing the cigarettes from the floor he sits on the sofa again. Taking the last cigarette he crumples the packet and throws it towards the corner where Lindsay is sitting. Jo, feeling awkward, stands and picks it up, straightening it out and putting it in her pocket.

'What are you doing?'

'It's got a number on it that I want.' She sits and swigs from her glass, hoping that the whisky will unbunch her neck.

'Probably some woman you picked up today. Hear that Lindsay? You bloody dykes are all the same, you never stop. I suppose anything will do, you're so desperate.'

'Shut up Simon, you're pathetic.'

'And you two aren't?'

'Just shut up, you're making a fool of yourself.'

'Who cares?'

The three of them slump in their chairs, having reached the end of the first round. Simon laughs to himself and stares at Lindsay, who has bowed her head. He laughs once more, wanting either of them to ask him what he finds funny; neither do. Lindsay, finishing her drink, puts the glass on the floor.

'Simon we're going to have to talk about money at some point. I'm going to the bank tomorrow and withdraw from the joint account what's mine. Obviously I'll split the bills for this month and the quarterly ones. I know you won't want to go through all this now, but I ought to let you know what I'm doing.'

'Bit late for that isn't it?'

'You can keep the furniture and stuff. I'm just taking my clothes.'

'You're really going to do this?'

'Yes. I've told you that often enough, you just wouldn't listen.'

'You're going to go now, this evening?'

'Yes. There's no point in my staying, is there?'

'Don't go. I'm sure we can sort something out. Don't take her, Jo, please.'

'It's up to Lindsay, not me.' Something is spiralling, here, in this room. Twisting to an unknown end. She wants to stop it. But how?

'Lindsay, please stay. I don't understand what's happening. Is it something I've done? I'm sorry.' Simon is crying again, his eyes swollen, almost unseeing.

'No, it's nothing you've done. It's just that something's changed, I love Jo and I want to be with her. It's not that I don't love you, I just don't love you in the same way as before.'

Simon is sucked into the vortex, swept away by rage. He springs up from the sofa and kicks a table across the tiny room. Spinning round he sweeps books to the floor from a shelf. Jo signals to Lindsay to get out but she herself stays, knowing she must. She sits immobile, not wanting to attract Simon's fury which will burn itself out in seconds. Jo does not know how she knows these things. The man on the other side of the room falls to his knees slowly, to assume an attitude of supplication. Jo stands very slowly and walks over to sit next to him, putting her arm around his shoulder. Simon slumps against her, resting his head on her chest. She thinks how awkward the position is and how she will have to stay like this until he moves. She strokes his hair, saying nothing. They sit huddled on the floor until he stops sobbing. Gently Jo takes her arm away. Her neck seizes up again and she waits for it to relax.

'Stay here I won't be a moment.'

Walking past the kitchen she glances to see Lindsay, who she loves, sitting at the table unmoving. Is she unmoved? Once in the bedroom Jo stuffs clothes into the suitcases and whips through the wardrobes, taking out all the clothes she knows to be Lindsay's. Crudely jamming everything into small spaces left in various bags, she fastens them and carries them out to the hall. This done she returns to the living room, the chaos there striking her for the first time. There is nothing left on the shelves, records have been smashed, glasses broken. Simon sits where he did before. Jo goes over and kneels down in front of him.

'Simon. Come on, come with me. Stand up.' She eases him up, hands under his armpits, taking the full weight of him as he staggers upright. She leads him from the room and down the passage to the bedroom. Pulling back the covers she lets him fall on the bed. She takes off his shoes and socks and then pulls him into sitting position, floppy as a rag doll, to take off his jumper. Strangely, she hears her mother's voice: 'Less of the spaghetti legs, miss.' Always, when she was a child her legs would become rubbery at the thought of having to put on wellington boots. Her mother had had to stuff two tiny bits of rubber into the boots and then pull her to her rubber feet. Jo finds herself smiling and is amazed. Letting Simon fall back again, she covers him with the bedclothes. Immediately he rolls over and tucks himself into a ball, hands crossed under his chin.

'I'll be back in a minute. Go to sleep now.'

In the kitchen Lindsay has not moved. Both she and Simon have wound down the spiral and reached the point of inertia. Gathering herself together for one last effort, Jo goes over to her and kisses her on the cheek.

'It's alright, I think he's asleep now.'

'I can't leave him like this.'

'I know. But you can't stay either.'

'What are we going to do? Both stay here?'

'No, I'll phone one of his friends and ask them to come over and stay with him. Or maybe you should. Do you know anyone who'd do that?'

'Um. Let me think. Yes there is someone, if he's in. A bloke called Dirk, who he went to school with, he lives near here and I know they're very good friends.'

'Right, where's his number?'

'I'll find it. I think it's in Simon's diary.'

Exhausted, Jo slumps onto a chair, staring at her hands. Equal to both giving and taking. Her right hand is hurting. It lies on the table, red and white, blood and skin. I feel that I am running out of blood. I don't have much time left during which I can hold myself together. Please let this be over soon. Pulling out the cigarette packet she remembers it is empty and sits staring at the number scrawled on it. Red and white, it smiles at her.

'Here it is. Will you phone, or shall I?'

'I think,' drawing breath, 'that you should.'

'What shall I say?'

'Just say that you and Simon have had an argument, that you're leaving him, that he's in a state and you don't want to leave him alone. But you can't stay. In short, the truth.' Deceit needing energy.

'O.K. Do you think he'll do it?'

'How should I know?'

Jo hauls herself up and goes back to the bedroom. Simon has not moved since she left the room. Going over, she checks that he is indeed asleep. In the light from the hallway, she picks out his face, placid now. She wishes there were a way to wash his mind, to launder the images of this dreadful day so that he might wake unchanged. But there is nothing she can do. Hearing the phone being put down, she leaves Simon alone and closes the door quietly.

The two women meet in the hall.

'It's O.K. He said he'd come over.'

'How long will he be?'

'Not long. He only lives round the corner. He said about twenty minutes.'

'Good.' There is no room for affection here, now. There is no room for words of love or assurance as we wrap up this messy parcel, only to leave it on a stranger's doorstep. 'Is there any food here, I mean so that they can have something later?'

'Yes. There's milk and everything.' All laid in for an emotional siege.

'O.K. Well, I've got all your stuff, I think. At least, enough for a while, until you can come back and collect anything else you want.' Watching Lindsay, Jo can see that she is about to break down. 'Do you want to see this bloke, Dirk?'

'No, I don't. I don't think he likes me anyway, and he sounded really annoyed on the phone.'

'Why don't you wait in the car and I'll meet him. It won't take long. Did you tell him about me?'

'No, I thought it was better not to.' Truth – yes, but only so much.

'That'll be alright then. Let's put your bags in the car.'

'I will be coming back, won't I?' There is fear in Lindsay's voice as she grabs Jo's arm.

'What for?'

'For my other stuff.'

'If you want to.'

'There's so much of it here. Little things. I've lived here for years. Four years. Did I tell you?'

'Yes, yes, you told me.'

'Come on, quick. Let's take out the stuff.' Lindsay's hair is slipping out of the grips at the back of her neck and is framing her face. Her face: taut and helpless, as Jo has never seen it before.

The bags loaded, Lindsay stands in the road, by the car. Jo feels she is saying goodbye, waving her away. Will it come to that? Is that what I shall be doing one day? As Simon said?

'I'll be out when I've seen Dirk. Just wait in the car, he won't see you. I won't be long.' Lindsay climbs in and locks the doors as Jo knew she would. Once back inside, Jo looks for some aspirin to dull the dull thump in her temples. Not long now, she thinks, not long now. She has been ticking off the minutes, knowing that this is a race between her patience and time, unsure which will win. A knock at the front door gives her hope that she may yet. Opening it she fixes a smile on her face.

'Hello, are you Dirk?' Standing in the doorway

is a small, child-like figure, with dark hair and glasses.

'Yes, I've come to look after Simon. Where's Lindsay?' He peers over Jo's shoulder, standing on tiptoes.

'She's already gone. Come in.'

'Thank you.' He walks past her, his head reaching her shoulder. 'Where's Simon?'

'He's in there, asleep.'

'Asleep?'

'Yes. I think he's been drinking quite a lot today, that and the emotion have worn him out. But we didn't think he should be left alone.'

'What happened?'

'I don't know.'

'Good God, what the hell happened in here?' He looks around the living room at the mess and glances up at Jo.

'Simon, he was very upset and kind of lost control.'

'Christ, I didn't realise it was this bad.' The little man takes off his coat and kneels down to pick up some broken glass. His shirt is ironed and tucked into his pressed jeans. His hair is neatly parted, showing a line of newly washed skin. Jo watches this strict, collected person moving around the room, clearing the floor, putting tables and chairs where they should be. Minutes pass, with Jo following the restoration of order. Pulling herself out of a trance, she reaches for her jacket which, surprisingly, is still hanging on the chair.

'Well, I'd better get going. There's lots of food and stuff here, if you want anything. And there's some booze in the kitchen.'

'It's O.K. I know my way around quite well. In the flat I mean.'

'Good. Well ... thank you for doing this. For coming round.'

'That's O.K.'

'Bye then. I'll call tomorrow, or Lindsay will, to see how he is.'

'Bye.' Standing in the shattered room, they shake hands. The fight is over; the ring is being cleared.

Walking over to the car, Jo remembers the accident and sighs, she should have phoned the police hours ago, but it will have to wait. The number is safe in a pocket. Tapping on the window she startles Lindsay, who has been sitting with her eyes closed, thinking nothing. They sit next to each other in silence. For what is there to say? Eventually Jo drives off, back along the same roads as before. Nearing home she feels a weight lifting from her.

She will make it.

Still nothing has been said. Parking, she looks at Lindsay.

'Are you alright?' Jo touches Lindsay's shoulder.

'Yes, I suppose so. I just can't believe I've done it.'

'Come on. I'm knackered. Let's get in the house.'

The bulging bags are brought out of the boot, which groans as it opens, bent by the nameless men in their numbered car.

'What happened? I didn't notice that before.'

'It happened on the way to your place. Some bastards crashed into me as I was waiting at a roundabout. It's their registration number on the fag packet.'

Lindsay stops and looks at Jo, moving towards her. For the first time that day they touch, holding each other tightly in the middle of a dark, empty road. Jo can feel her lover shaking and hugs her even closer. This is the last thing I can do.

'Come on, let's go inside.' She leads Lindsay to the door and opens it. Once inside, she draws Lindsay to her and takes them both to the chair by the phone. Pulling the exhausted woman into her lap she rocks her slowly in silence. Still the lights flicker across the dark room, still the cars and buses rumble. Difficult, now, to think of what has happened, to think of the day that has gone. To imagine doing what was done, for I could not do it again. In another flat, not far from here, lies another person feeling towards the future. Can we put anything back, where it was? Can any of us build something from all this damage, this rubble? Moving away from this day, what will I remember? Could it have been different? Perhaps less cruel?

'Were you playing cards?' Lindsay mumbles in Jo's neck, noticing the table covered with numbers and faces and dots.

'Yes.'

'What were you playing?'

'It hasn't got a name. It's something I made up when I was a kid when I didn't have anything better to do.'

'Has it got rules?'

'Oh, yes, but only I know what they are. It's a game that only I can play.'

'Will you teach me?'

'I don't think I can.'

'Why's the ace lying there like that? Does that mean you've won?'

'Sometimes. But this is a game I haven't finished.'

They are both slipping into the warm, private world of the chair, wrapped around one another, giving in to the desire to sleep but wanting to speak the first words of a new life.

THE PIED PIPER: Lesbian Feminist Fiction

edited by Anna Livia & Lilian Mohin

Tales full or humour, high spirits, social comment, pathos and metaphor made flesh. The landscape changes as you move from one story to the next: medieval Britain, 19th century Jamaica, contemporary southern France, dyke bars in London and the States. These stories by lesbian feminist novelists, poets and playwrights rework classic themes and give us fresh departures: the teenage fag-hag, Blacklesbian myth and reality, the historical 'passing' woman and, of course, coming out and falling in love. An anthology whose hallmark is surprise and revelation.

A NOISE FROM THE WOODSHED

by Mary Dorcey

A collection of lesbian feminist short stories by an Irish author already revered as a poet. Her prose is by turns lyrical, ironic, sensual and exuberantly funny. In settings ranging from rural Ireland to a Roman summer to a London fallout shelter these stories include: the final scenes of a heterosexual marriage, scrupulous, tender and knowing lesbian 'romance', expatriate Irish lesbians dealing with British racism and an escape from an old-age asylum. This is fiction at once universal, feminist and especially Irish.

THE REACH: Lesbian Feminist Fiction

edited by Lilian Mohin & Sheila Shulman

Britain's first (1984) anthology of lesbian feminist short stories, in its third printing.

"old love affairs, saying goodbye to a dying grandfather, adolescent lesbian love, not making love and lesbian aunts, to name a few ... The stories are alternately puzzling, sad, funny and knowing. Unlike many anthologies, *The Reach* is consistently good, not at all uneven, and highly pleasing. This is the best lesbian-feminist fiction anthology I've ever seen. 4 stars."

off our backs

INCIDENTS INVOLVING WARMTH
lesbian feminist love stories

by Anna Livia

"Here are short stories that interpret love in many different ways. Passion, friendship, long term relationships, lust in the dust and what it means to become involved with straight women are all explored ... to find a book that's not drearily confessional, not coy, not salacious, but simply true and fertile, is like finding gourmet vegetarian dishes on the steakhouse menu."

Time Out

****

A free catalogue of radical feminist and lesbian books is available from: ONLYWOMEN PRESS, 38 Mount Pleasant, London WC1X 0AP, U.K.